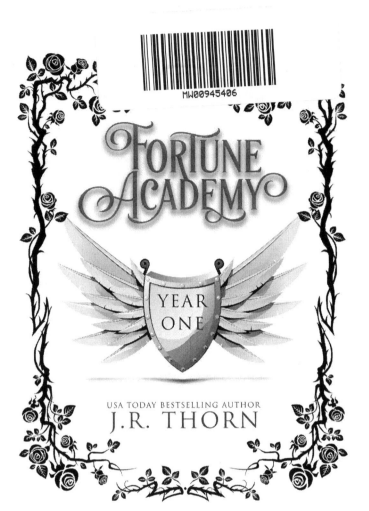

FORTUNE ACADEMY

YEAR ONE

USA TODAY BESTSELLING AUTHOR

J.R. THORN

Fortune Academy: Year One © 2019 by J.R. Thorn

Cover Art by "Covers by Juan"
Line Edit by Kristen Breanne
Love2ReadRomance Proofreading & Editing Service

ISBN: 9781688358737

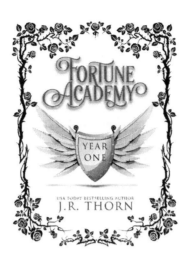

Welcome to Fortune Academy, a school where supernaturals can feel at home—except, I have no idea what the hell I am.

The last thing I remember is arriving at the massive gates with a Bounty Hunter staring me down. I have a feeling he was supposed to take me to the monster holding arena to fight and die. Instead, I'm Fortune Academy's newest student.

I can relate to the monsters in ways the other students can't. My mentor, who is way too hot for his own good, tells me my behavior is the result of my memory loss and that I'm just trying to identify with a past pain that I've buried too far to feel. I think he's wrong. I think the reason I can't relate to any of the students is because I'm one of the monsters they're trained to kill.

I don't fit into any of the supernatural cliques, but that doesn't stop me from collecting bullies. A brawny alpha shifter, a moody dark mage, and a playboy demigod have decided to break me. They think I don't have any powers and that I was recruited by mistake. It'll be their funeral if they push me too far, because this girl isn't taking any of their shit.

My name is Lily Fallen, but don't let my pretty face fool you. I'm a monster in a school uniform and it's only a matter of time before I teach my bullies a lesson they won't forget.

Fortune Academy: Year One is the first of three novels in a college-age paranormal academy series. Expect a slow-burn enemies-to-lovers romance where there are multiple guys and no choosing required!

CHAPTER 1

IT ALL STARTED WITH A SEVERED HAND AND A hot bounty hunter. For the record, I would never chop off the hand of a hot guy... unless he was being a total douchebag—which he was. Plus, it grew back, so it doesn't even really count... not that I was aware bounty hunters could regrow appendages, but hey, no harm no foul.

Right, I tend to blather on without context so let me start from the beginning, right around the time when my memories restarted in the middle of the street with no idea who I was. Boy, was I in for a surprise when I figured that one out.

The first thing I remember from that point on was my clothes sticking to my skin and my hair plastered to my cheeks from the freezing rain. Everything was sore as if I'd been run over by a bulldozer. I wandered, drawn by a pull that promised refuge until I found myself in a dark alley facing the back entrance of a bar. Raindrops hit my face like irritating little insects, but I couldn't seem to find the strength to leave this particular doorstep. Something bad had happened to me and I must have run until I couldn't run anymore. My legs trembled underneath me like jello and my heart wouldn't stop thundering in my ears. All I could do was gulp in breaths of air and wait for someone to open that dull, red door lined with scratches.

The moonlight was too bright, but I peered up at the sky and pleaded for mercy anyway. I didn't know what I needed mercy for, or why I was paralyzed in the freezing rain at this grimy doorstep, but I just knew that this was my last hope. I had to stay here until that door opened.

The streetlights blasted on and made me flinch, but I stared at the door until it opened and a woman in her late forties peered down at me with a disgusted scowl. She stared at me for a long time before she stepped aside. "Come on," she said, then turned around and left the entranceway free.

That's how I became Cindy's newest waitress. Waiting like a drowned rat at the back of her bar to what was supposed to be her secret entrance reserved for smoke breaks. Well, that's how all supernaturals found Cindy. Now when I walked outside I could spot the little ugly engraving in the corner of the doorway that drew people like me to the place. A little tiny skull etched there with a dumb grin on its face like it knew how many headaches it would bring Cindy. This was her punishment... to help people like me who had no memory of who they were or what they'd done. Ever since the Second Echo of Calamity apparently the world had gone to all sorts of shit and supernaturals had to start over with clean slates, memories included. What Cindy had done to deserve her fostering of looney supernaturals, I had no idea and she wasn't about to admit it to me.

The thing was, Cindy attracted just that, supernaturals. Sure, something was off about me, but even I felt like I didn't quite fit in with the supernatural crowd of misfits. I had a feeling that my memory loss didn't have much to do with the whacky weirdness that was going on with the world. It was something more personal... but Cindy didn't have to know that.

I liked Cindy. She never asked questions or gave me a hard time when I didn't seem to know basic things. It felt like I had to learn how to live life all over again. Something fundamental had changed in me and I couldn't put my finger on what. Without having any memory of my past, I wasn't even going to try and figure it out. Let it come naturally, that's what Cindy always said.

We had this weird kind of understanding that made our relationship work. I'd shown up on her doorstep in the middle of the night covered in blood and soaked with rain and she'd taken me in just like she'd done with so many before me.

That's what the mother of monsters always did.

"Guy at table three has been ogling you for an hour," Jess told me as she balanced a tray on her hip.

Jess was the closest thing I had to a friend in the same way that Cindy was the closest thing I had to a mother. Jess had arrived only a few weeks before I did, but she was already well on her way to recovery. Cindy had set up a few interviews for Jess at various escort gigs. Normally I'd disapprove, but Jess seemed to love the attention, so I hoped she would be happy when it was time for her to go.

"Don't be a bimbo," I said, making a point to ignore the guy she'd pointed out. "No way he's looking at me when you're standing right here." I gave her short skirt and halter top a raised brow. She already had voluptuous boobs and a rounded ass big enough to make a guy stop in his tracks, and that outfit made everything pop in just the right way. "I'm not a succubus like you."

She grinned, showing off her pearly white teeth. "I'm serious, Lily, he's checking you out!"

Dread washed over me. I had the good looks, sure. Long, blonde hair, legs that could kill in some heels and plump lips that would be perfect for pouting... if I ever

4

pouted, which I didn't. I desperately hoped that I wasn't a succubus.

I still didn't know what I was yet, which was frustrating, but since being a succubus was still on the table I scanned the bar just for good measure. Every guy in the place was drooling over Jess and making a fool of themselves... every guy except for the one at table three.

Our gazes matched long enough for a jolt of familiar awareness to slam through me.

Okay, that was weird.

I tried to pretend I was fascinated with my phone. "I'm off duty, Jess," I reminded her as I scrolled through a mindless social media thread. "Go give the guy a new beer. The one you gave him an hour ago looks flat and he's probably just thirsty."

"Yeah," she snickered and waggled her eyebrows, "thirsty for some of your lo-ove," she said, making sure to sing-song the last word.

Ignoring her, I continued to scroll through my phone. It wasn't hard to pretend my fascination when the damn thing was so addictive. Cindy allowed me to use it as long as it was only for "research," as she called it. I never called anyone or posted anything online. I loved to read about humans and see what kinds of things they shared with each other. Most of it involved vague statements I didn't understand, pictures of kittens—which I always approved of—and snaps of perfectly arranged meals. Then there was the occasional political post about the emergence of supernaturals. Everyone had an opinion, especially when it came to Fortune Academy. *A Place Where Supernaturals Belong.* That was their slogan.

When I'd asked Cindy about it, she'd sneered and told me that if I was smart, I'd steer clear of anything related to that place.

Not that I was going to tell Cindy my opinion, but she had to be wrong. An entire organization dedicated to helping lost supernaturals? While I appreciated all that Cindy did for me, she didn't have answers. Fortune Academy would give me a fighting chance at figuring out what the hell I was.

One slight problem... the academy had stringent perquisites to join, one of which is demonstrating a supernatural ability—which I hadn't been able to do yet. I only knew I was supernatural because I'd lost my memories and Cindy's door rune had called me to her.

I'd figure out what I was... but it wasn't going to be easy.

Jess elbowed me in the ribs. "Hey, are you listening to me?"

I rolled my eyes. "You're still here? I said I was busy."

She leaned in and lowered her voice, not taking her eyes off the stranger. "I really think you should go talk to him, Lils. I can tell when a guy has the hots, and while he definitely has the hots for you, something is off about him that I can't really figure out. I don't like it."

I chuckled. "I'll tell you what's off about him. There's a gorgeous succubus in the room and he's staring at me. Clearly the guy's missing some marbles." And of course she didn't like it. Jess needed to get all of the male attention—which was fine with me.

"Hey, sweet cheeks!" A guy from across the bar yelled at Jess. "You bringing me those beers, or what?"

Jess waved at him and giggled, which just pissed me off. "You should go kick that guy in the balls."

Jess huffed and readjusted her tray. "That's not how I get the good tips. Now go talk to the hottie at table three or I will." She pursed her lips and gave me a you-better-go-talk-to-him-or-else look and then marched over to deliver the impatient human his beers.

I turned my attention back to the topic of our discussion. The stranger hunched into himself, hiding his face in the shadow of his cowl. I frowned.

That either meant he was shy, or he was hiding something.

Someone who could resist a succubus' charms wasn't the shy type, so I stuffed my phone in the back of my jeans pocket and marched over to his table. I crossed my arms until he grunted at me.

"Oh, so you can talk?" I snapped. Irritation put me on edge. I was standing right in front of him and he

7

wouldn't look up at me. "What, you can stare at me all night when I'm halfway across the room but when I come to your table you've got nothing to say?"

He twisted the untouched beer that Jess had delivered to him an hour ago, leaving a ring of condensation on the table. "So, you don't remember me." His voice came out husky and low... and apparently he knew who I was.

My entire body froze and a cold sweat broke out on my face. I'd harbored the secret hope that someone might recognize me in a popular bar, but I'd also feared the day someone who knew me might show up. I'd arrived at a monster's orphanage... and I'd been soaked in more than icy rain that night I'd shown up at Cindy's doorstep.

Yes I'd been covered in blood—but it was blood that wasn't my own. By the time I got my clothes off that night and slipped into a borrowed set of pajamas, I discovered I didn't have a single scratch on me.

I somehow managed to swallow the bitter fear that crawled up my throat. Letting out a nervous laugh, I flipped my hair over my shoulder. Guys always reacted better when they thought I was a dumb blonde. "Sorry. Maybe if you weren't hiding behind your cowl I could actually see your face, you know? Hard to jostle the memory with just a broody voice."

He hesitated and then shifted so that his cowl moved

just enough for me to see the hard ridge of his chin. "I don't brood," he growled.

It was almost cute how he immediately retorted the insult. I was about to make it worse, but then he pulled back his hood all the way and hot damn, the guy was smoking.

And, well, his eyes glowed with a metallic orange magic that marked him as a supernatural bounty hunter... but yeah, details.

I shouldn't have been surprised that a bounty hunter would show up at Cindy's bar, but he still managed to take me off guard. While my mind was mush, my body reacted to the deadly flash of silver that was his blade. The world around me stilled with a magical lock. I didn't know if it was something I'd done or if it had been the bar's defenses. Taking advantage of the moment, I twisted to put as much distance as possible between me and the hunter.

Except... he tracked my movements with ease, his eyes locked onto mine as I moved. When I flinched, he flicked the blade and its merciless silver etched across my vision. I knew it would be sharp enough to cut my head clean off my body, but I realized a half-second too late that he hadn't been aiming for me.

Jess cried out and clutched at the embedded hilt, crumpling to the floor as time unlocked from its slowed momentum.

"Jess!" I screamed and lurched to her aid, but the hunter had me by the arm with a vice grip.

"You're welcome," he growled and tugged me into his chest. "She was about to kill you."

Flattened against his hard abs, I curled my fingers into the thick layers of his coat and peered up at him, taking in the full brutal force of his hard edges and glowing eyes. Everything about him screamed danger, but the way he held me was protective... almost gentle.

A clatter of metal hit the floor and broke a silence that I realize didn't make any sense in a crowded bar. No one seemed to notice that Jess had been stabbed, or that a hunter with glowing eyes was holding me.

That was because time was frozen... but not Jess.

Jess... who now had a dagger plunged in her chest.

Even a succubus should have died from a mortal wound like that, but she snarled as if irritated by the blade and launched for me. The hunter reacted before I did and held out his hand to defend me, which would have been sweet, except the weapon struck clean through flesh and bone, severing his hand and sending it flopping to the floor like a lump of meat.

"Oh dear..." I murmured.

He cursed and wrapped the stumped remains of his hand in his cloak. When Jess cried out and collapsed to her knees, I realized that he hadn't cursed under his breath, but rather cast a spell.

So, my bounty hunter had some magical mojo.

"You bastard!" Jess screamed. "She's mine!"

My brain couldn't process Jess screaming at the hunter, so my gaze wandered throughout the bar that was like a snapshot in time.

A group three tables down held up their beers in celebration and one sloshed his contents into the air, the foam and droplets making a perfect arc over his friend's head.

Cars outside that should have been speeding down the dark alleyway were now stopped. The one closest to the window featured a woman with her hair fanned out behind her as if she was trapped in a photoshoot.

Then I spotted Cindy watching from the back with the door cracked open. Even she was trapped in the moment. Whatever had frozen time, only the hunter, Jess, and I were able to move. It bothered me more that Cindy was just back there... watching... as if waiting for something to happen. If she knew who the hunter was, why wouldn't she have stopped me from talking to him?

The hunter shook me with his remaining hand. He should have been buckled over in pain, but I didn't know much about bounty hunters. Maybe he could shut his pain off. "You need to stop daydreaming," he snapped. "Look." He pointed and my gaze obeyed even though my brain didn't want to process what was going on.

A knife rested on the ground just inches from Jess's hand, but not the one the hunter had stabbed her with. That one was still lodged in her chest and blood pooled around the wound and seeped into her clothing.

"Jess?" I asked, my voice cracking when I finally realized that she'd been coming at us with a knife. Not just any knife, but a blade etched with runes that glowed red.

I considered Jess my friend, even though I'd only been here a few weeks and was still trying to remember who I was. Cindy told me that I shouldn't rush it. Just take as much time as I needed. Jess had always been supportive in her own way, but this wasn't the Jess who talked to me about guys or stole a shot with me from behind the bar. She gripped the hilt of the dagger still embedded in her chest and glared at me. I'd never seen anyone look at me with such hatred, much less someone I thought was my friend.

"You're a monster," she said, almost like it was something she'd kept in for far too long. "You're supposed to work for us. No one else can have you!" She lurched for the dagger she'd dropped, but cried out in pain and slapped her hand on the floor.

If it hadn't been for the hunter who still held me with one strong arm, I would have gone ice cold. I hadn't been in many situations where I was this stressed, but sometimes when a customer got rowdy or Cindy raised her voice my fingertips would go so cold that they'd feel numb until I grabbed onto someone. Now the urge to touch devoured me worse than I'd ever felt it and I crawled my hands up the hunter's clothes until I reached a patch of skin exposed at his neck. He flinched the moment my icy fingers met his, but he didn't stop me. Instead he stroked my hair out of my eyes and gave me a sobering look.

"It's Lily, right?"

Hearing my name jolted me into awareness and I looked into his eyes that still glowed with that fascinating metallic golden gleam. "Uh, yeah." How did he know my name?

He surveyed the bar and frowned. "I can't hold the time lock once we step outside of this bar. We're lucky that the monster mother was on the other side of the door when I initiated it." He glanced down at the dagger still in Jess's chest. I noticed one gem on the end of the hilt glowing green, but that light was starting to fade. "We don't have much longer. Do you think you can move?"

The shock of what he was proposing made all the heat I'd gathered into my fingertips surge straight through my whole body. He jerked away from me and cursed.

"You can't mean that I'd go somewhere with you?" I asked.

"Yes," he growled, transforming from the kind and

patient stranger I'd been clinging to back into the hunter that had come to... what had he come here to do? "If you stay here you'll be killed... or worse. You have to come with me."

Sense came back to me as I bristled. No one told me what to do. "I can take care of myself, thank you very much."

"You better listen to him," Jess drawled, grinning manically as her eyelids drooped and blood tinted her teeth pink. It was the most terrifying sight I'd ever seen, especially since one side of her face was starting to droop and one of her eyes was turning black. "I'm not really a succubus, you know. I'm something else... something even better. I wasn't ready to show you, but looks like I don't have a choice. You lost your memory because you weren't ready to learn what you are, but I've embraced it."

"You shut your mouth," the hunter snapped and produced a second blade. "Lily is nothing like you."

She gurgled on another laugh. "Oh, protective, are you? Didn't come to kill her... but to collect her for your little academy? How quaint."

I dug my fingernails into my palm. The air around us started to tremble as if the whole world was about to fall apart. I couldn't leave Jess here, dying, even if she was frightening me. I didn't care what she was, I needed to give her a chance to explain. Maybe if she thought I wouldn't go with him she'd stop trying to attack me.

She gave me a look of pity. Which was incredulous. Jess, the one with the knife in her chest and her face falling apart, gave *me* a look of pity. "Such a sweet thing. You still want to help me, don't you?" She sighed. "Tricky blood you have. Two-thirds of you is perfect for Monster Academy, but there's that nasty little extra third that shows its ugly head. I see it right now in your eyes. No proper monster would look at me like that." Her face twisted with rage. "Mother will burn it out of you. Then you can join us and Monster Academy will finally have its star pupil." She chuckled. "Or failed experiment. Either way, I will be getting some major extra credit for this."

"Monster Academy?" I shrieked. "Jess, what the hell are you talking about?"

She opened her mouth to answer me, but a loud crack reverberated through the room and time unlocked from its latch.

"Time to go," the hunter said and took me by the arm again.

Everything happened all at once. The serene silence dropped into a clatter of noise typical of a busy bar. Startled, I ducked as if the bombardment of sounds was an object hurled at my head, and good thing, too. Cindy

burst through the door and launched fire—fucking fire!
—from her hand.

I'd never seen anything like it. The flames were so hot
that they melted straight through a pair of guests and
sent their corpses disintegrating to the floorboards. The
bar exploded and the scent of fear hit me like a wall.

"Come on!" the hunter shouted and tugged at me,
but I was rooted to the spot. He gave me a look of
surprise.

That's right. I was supernatural. No fucking idea
what I was, but he wasn't going to move me unless I
agreed to it.

Which, going with him was starting to feel like a
good idea. Jess was talking about hooking me up with
Monster Academy—no idea what that was but it didn't
sound good—and Cindy was throwing fire around and
killing people.

I had a decision to make and not much time to make
it. One quick glance at Jess gave me mixed feelings. She
clearly wasn't a succubus. Jess's beauty melted off of her
as if the dagger in her chest drained her of her outer skin.
I wasn't sure if it had been a spell or some elaborate
magical sleeve, but whatever this creature was before me
now with black eyes and wrinkled skin was the real Jess.

Strangely, I wanted to get to know her. Those black
eyes still had Jess inside of them. There was more dark-

ness and pain, but still the friend that I'd come to care for.

Yet, when she went for the cool blade again on the floor, I knew that she would rather kill me than let the hunter have me. Perhaps I was naive, just like she always told me I was.

Closing my eyes with resignation, I let the hunter haul me out of the bar and into the cold night.

Of course, it was fucking raining, and the blood on me wasn't my own.

TO BE A MONSTER

Jess had said so many things that had me reeling and I just wanted time to process it all.

Unfortunately, time only stood still when Mr. Bounty Hunter cast his voodoo magic. He must have been all out of the stuff, because he dragged me through the dark streets as if the hounds of hell were on our tails. All I could do was gulp in breaths of air as we fled through endless alleyways until I was hopelessly lost.

"Will you slow down? No one is following us," I said through my chattering teeth. The rain had seeped through my thin clothes I normally wore in the stuffy bar and that frostbite feeling was back. I drew heat from where our hands touched, grateful that he didn't let go of me even as we ran.

If he heard me, then he was doing a good job of ignoring me. Maybe Jess was right. Maybe the hunter was going to take me to my doom or something far worse. Her voice rang clear in my head.

You're a monster.

You're supposed to work for us.

Then she'd mentioned the academy... the hunter had come looking for me, but if I was really like Jess, if I was really a monster, then I belonged in a place like Monster Academy.

Not Fortune Academy.

None of this made any sense and I needed some damn answers. There was nothing fortunate about being a monster. If I'd really lost my memories because of some horror of what I was, then I had no desire to discover that part of myself, but I had a feeling that a hunter wouldn't come track me down unless he thought I was special.

Having enough of the hunter's endless plight—as well as the panic threatening to take over my thoughts —I yanked as hard as I could on his grip, making him falter. He blinked at me with his mesmerizing orange eyes as if stunned I'd had the strength to stop him. I grinned. If I really was a monster, then at least there were some perks if it made him look at me like that twice in one night. He wasn't going to push me around.

"All right," I began, "you're going to stop dragging me through the rain and tell me where we are going." I kept my voice steady in spite of the chill rolling spasms through my jaw.

The hunter rolled his eyes and tried to shake his hand free of mine, but I didn't dare let go. If I did, I was afraid I'd really freeze to death. He was so warm and it felt like he was my only tether to life.

He glowered at me, but stopped trying to reclaim his hand. "I'm taking you to Fortune Academy, of course," he said, irritation growling on the edges of his words.

"Yes," I said, taking a step closer to him, "I got that much, but what are we going to do when we get there? If what Jess said is true—"

He yanked me in close until I flattened against his chest, making me squeak in surprise. His words caressed over me, angry, but I had the feeling his anger wasn't directed at me. "That demonspawn said a lot of things, but I don't pay much attention to her kind, and you shouldn't either."

I swallowed hard as my once icy cheeks flamed with new heat. "You make it sound like I'm different." I ran one hand down his arm, the one where he'd lost a hand saving me from Jess's blade. "You protected me..." I drew back the cloth to see how much damage there was. No matter what kind of supernatural creature he might be, he needed to properly bandage a wound like that.

I gasped when the bloodied cloth fell away and

revealed pink fingers. He flexed the appendage and gave me a seductive smirk.

"My gods," I whispered. "Did your hand... grow back?"

He shrugged as if he regrew lost appendages every day. "Perk of the job, I guess," he muttered and held his new hand up to the moonlight. A faint red line wrapped around his wrist—a scar that proved he'd protected me... a monster.

I ran my fingers over the raised line. "Will the scar heal, too?"

He flinched away from me and his hand disappeared into the folds of his jacket. "Scars don't heal."

Almost the instant he said it I noticed the fine raised lines that etched across his otherwise flawless skin. He was covered with the soft lines that betrayed how much he'd already been through. Perhaps it was the magnetizing pull of his metallic orange eyes that kept me fixated enough I hadn't noticed the groove that ran down his cheek, or the long slice that ran horizontally across his throat. I shivered. "Who did that to you?"

He rolled his eyes as if I'd asked a ridiculous question. "I'm a Monster Hunter, that means I hunt creatures that don't want to be hunted."

"Pretty sure no one wants to be hunted," I grumbled.

He glowered at me, which had an extra dollop of

intoxication when his eyes glowed like that. I wasn't sure, but it seemed like they were brighter. I decided that it either meant I was pissing him off, or his magical reserves were rejuvenating.

Then I realized that we weren't touching anymore, thanks to that icy feeling at the back of my neck. I reached out on instinct and took his hand again and the fresh surge of warmth swept through our touch, banishing the growing cold in my chest. "This rain is so damn cold," I complained. "Why aren't you cold like me?"

He looked at me as if he wanted to say something, but he pinched his lips together before tugging me closer to him. "I know you have questions and there will be time for answers, but right now I need to get you out of danger."

"Pretty sure you're the one in danger," I pointed out.

Ignoring me, he knelt and drew out his blade. It's not like I knew the guy. Any sane person would have backed away from the supernatural with a weapon, but I knelt down with him and leaned in close, making sure to keep one hand on his forearm so that I could steal some of his heat. The rain got in my eyes and seemed to want to slither under my skin, but the hunter's warmth kept the cold intrusion at bay.

He took the blade and etched the sharp end along the ground, leaving a glowing line of red as if he could make cement itself bleed. My eyes widened. "Is that a spell?"

He grunted at me. "Yes, I'm making a portal so that we can get into Fortune Academy."

Portal. We were going to travel to the academy in a... portal. "Is that the only way to get there?" I asked, my voice rising a pitch. I knew that I belonged in the supernatural world, but I'd already experienced a time freeze, fireballs, and watching a man with glowing eyes regrow a chopped off appendage.

His fascinating eyes narrowed on me. "There's always a backdoor, even to a place like Fortune Academy. Now be quiet so I can focus."

The rain around us clattered on rooftops and beat against the alleyway. I found the storm much more distracting than I could ever be, but I obeyed and watched him as he worked. A pattern of glowing red marks traced after his blade and he paused at the end of each one, seeming to consider the next line before he started it. I'd never seen anyone draw lines so carefully. Almost as if... this wasn't how he normally ventured to Fortune Academy. "Is that line supposed to be straight?" I asked, suddenly nervous that perhaps he wasn't used to this method.

He glared at me. "Are you seriously going to backseat drive my portal spell?"

"Only because you're using a back door. Why can't we go in the same way everybody else does?"

I'd read enough on social media to get the gist. Fortune Academy even had a website, although they tended to be cryptic about how one actually joined the academy after getting approved. They had one single application page with the first question being multiple-choice, "Select Your Supernatural Affinity," with a long list of supernatural terms. I never knew what to put... and that was for the first question. They didn't have an "other" selection.

The next row asked for an ID number corresponding to a blood sample. They had a link to the approved facilities where one could donate a blood sample for application. Even if I knew what I was, for some reason I wasn't comfortable with giving a blood sample. I'd been putting it off until more of my memories came back.

The point was, it was clear that one did not sneak into a place like Fortune Academy. At least, not without some risk.

"Look," the hunter said, surprising me with a measure of patience that he let slide into his voice. "I'll explain everything, but you're going to have to trust me. I can't take you in the front door, but I can't leave you here, either. This is the best way to make sure you're safe."

I didn't know why a bounty hunter would care about keeping me safe, unless there was, well, a bounty for him to collect. I pushed my lower lip out and then sucked it between my teeth. "Asking for trust is a bit much right now, don't you think?"

He opened his mouth to reply, but a crash behind us made us both jump. I whirled just in time to see a very pissed-off Cindy barreling down the alleyway. "Ungrateful brat! I take you into my home, put a roof over your head, and you run off with the first recruiter that sniffs you out? I found you first!"

As much fun as Cindy looked like she might be with all the fireballs still launching from her fists and smoke pouring out of her ears, I clung to the hunter and decided if I had to trust someone, it was going to be him. Even if he was going to turn me into someone for a bounty, it would be at Fortune Academy. He'd called Cindy the "Mother of Monsters," and Jess had said that I belonged at "Monster Academy." It didn't take a genius to figure out who was the bad guy in this scenario... at least, I hoped so, anyway. Right now I needed answers and a place where my life wasn't in immediate danger. If I had to place a bet, my bet would be I'd have better survivability at Fortune Academy with a bounty hunter who wanted to keep me alive rather than Cindy who looked like she'd rather kill me than let anyone else get their hands on me.

Which meant... I wasn't just a supernatural, I was something that other supernaturals wanted.

Even if I didn't know what it was, I had power on my side which gave me enough confidence to lean closer to the hunter. "You're almost done, right?"

"Yep," he said under his breath and then hurried with a few more scratches, completing the pattern of runes. The last swipe sent the whole array alight with bright orange and red streaks as if the street itself had been set on fire. I jumped back with a squeal, but the hunter grabbed my wrist and tugged me onto the blazing platform. "Trust me!" he yelled.

Maybe not for the right reasons, or maybe Cindy's fire blazing behind me was a lot more frightening than the glowing runes at my feet, but in that moment, I trusted the hunter with my life.

Nothingness. It's not what I expected when stepping through a magical portal, but that's the only way to describe the sensation of floating and emptiness as I drifted alongside the hunter.

He marched forward with purpose, seemingly unbothered by the void that closed in all around us. I opened my mouth to speak, but no words came out. It seemed that there was a "no talking" rule in the world of nothing.

This was a place of in-between. It didn't feel like Earth, but I knew we weren't at Fortune Academy yet either. The portal bore a tunnel to our destination and it seemed like a safe, although creepy, method of transportation.

Minus the gaping hole with glowing red fire at the bottom of it. Details.

My hunter paused in front of the chasm and frowned. He glanced at me, his eyes glowing brighter than ever with their metallic hue. I didn't like the sweeping resolve that settled over his features.

He backed us up and crouched as he nodded towards the chasm.

No. Fuck no. We were not going to jump that—

I tried to scream, but the void swallowed up any hint of sound as the hunter launched us towards the pit. He bent his knees right at the edge and sprang with me behind him.

I knew that resisting would only increase our chances of falling into the chasm, so I put all my effort into my legs to propel with him. It made our flight easier, to my relief, as we sailed over the roiling sea of molten lava. I didn't want to know what that thing was and I certainly didn't want to fall into it and find out.

The edge of blackness welcomed us on the other side and the hunter landed first. My foot caught the rim and I went tumbling backwards, but he wasn't going to let me fall. Strong arms hauled me into his chest and we collapsed in a heap on the other side.

We fell into the safety of the blackness and a veil swept over me with a tingling promise that everything was going to be all right.

My ears popped and the dull sounds of a living world made me let out the breath I'd been holding.

"Holy shit," I said and rolled onto my side, finally unclenching my fingers from the hunter's arms. I expected the cold to rush back into me when I let go of him, but I felt okay. I thumped my head against the ground and sprawled out, not caring what I was lying on. I stared up at a foreign sky that would have looked familiar with its sprinkling of stars if it didn't have two moons. "You rushed those last few lines," I complained. "I told you they weren't straight."

He shrugged. "The tunnel was pretty solid minus that last obstacle, but it was kind of fun, don't you say?"

I rolled my eyes. "Yeah, fun. Let's go with that." Sighing, I let my gaze sweep over the dual moons that glowed down onto us. "Where are we?"

The hunter knelt and wrapped his knife in a cloth. It pulsed with angry red flashes of light. "We're here."

I rolled my eyes at him. "I can see that, but where is 'here?'"

He shrugged. "I don't think I could answer that even if I wanted to." He tucked his wrapped blade into his cloak and settled onto his knees. He watched me, his glowing eyes searching mine as his lips ticked up on the side. "I figured bringing you to Fortune Academy would make you feel better. There's color in your cheeks. It suits you."

I blushed at the compliment, which made me blush even more. I didn't... blush. Blushing was for people who

29

didn't get cold like I did or have any control over their basic biological impulses, which I was usually pretty solid on. I rubbed my fingers against my cheeks, hoping that the icy appendages would steal some of the heat, but to my surprise my fingers weren't cold like they normally were. Instead I felt warm all over... and I wasn't sure I liked it.

"What's wrong with me?"

His smirk grew into a full-out grin, making soft dimples form at his cheeks. "There's nothing wrong with you, but I think it's best if we get you to Kaito. I promised him that he'd get to fill you in on things."

I shot up, which I immediately regretted as dizziness swept over me. I rubbed my temples with slow, deliberate circles. "Who's Kaito?" I squinted one eye at him. "Actually, you never even gave me your name."

The hunter grunted and got to his feet. He offered me his hand, the one still slightly pink with a new scar that ran completely around his wrist. "Dante."

Of course, my hunter would have a name like Dante. "I don't know," I grumbled, taking his hand and allowing him to help me up. "That sounds kind of intimidating. How about Danny?"

His eyes flashed. "It's Dante."

With that apparently decided, he dragged me down the smooth streets that were lined with impressive gardens and even more impressive buildings.

"I bet this place looks amazing in the daytime," I said, unable to resist the urge to marvel that I was actually in Fortune Academy. "It looks even more amazing than the photos on the website." There weren't many, just enough to hint at a stunning infrastructure that would put colleges like Yale or Harvard to shame. While prestige on Earth was built on history, architecture, and tradition, Fortune Academy was built on magic.

Each building glowed with a life of its own, emanating power that sang through my veins. It was as if I'd been suffocating all my life and this was the first time I'd had a breath of fresh air. I drew in a long gulp and sighed.

Dante chuckled and twined his fingers through mine. Maybe that should have felt weird that we were holding hands, but I had a feeling that he didn't want me running off. I was still his bounty and holding hands was better than him holding me by my scruff like a mutt he'd tracked down in the streets. Whether it was intended to be friendly or not, I decided I liked holding hands with him. There was the faintest trickle of essence that fueled him and seeped into me through our touch. Even if I didn't completely understand it, I knew this had to be something to do with my supernatural powers. The only way I was going to understand them was if I just went with it.

"Kaito said you'd feel better once I got you here."

Dante straightened as he led me to one of the shorter buildings that glowed with the same golden orange as his eyes. "As much as I hate to admit it, he's normally right."

I gave the building a wary glance. Minus the light from its magical aura, I couldn't see any signs of life through its windows. We reached the doors and they opened with a mechanical swish that sent my hair unfurling over my shoulders. Even though I knew we were in a magical realm, it all felt oddly... normal.

I never liked walking around places at night. It was too quiet, too undisturbed. I like bustle and business, which is why I felt at home at Cindy's bar. The pang of regret that surged through my chest surprised me. It's not like I owed Cindy anything. Sure, she took me in, but she'd had her own agenda and plans for me. Never mind the fact that she'd tried to kill me... Jess too.

But without my memories, that bar had been the closest thing I'd had to a home. It had given me Cindy, the only person who knew what I'd been through, and Jess, the only person that I could talk about... anything with.

"Hey," Dante said, softly bringing me back to the present. "I know this is a lot to take in, but Kaito is a lot better at this sort of thing than I am. He'll make every-thing okay. That's what he does."

To be honest, Dante was doing a pretty good job of making me feel reassured, even though alarm bells were going off telling me that this Kaito guy was probably the person who was supposed to pay off my bounty. For now, though, I would play along. "You sure he's going to be here?" I asked. "It seems like the whole place is sleeping."

Dante tugged me along with him and I followed. "He'll be waiting up for us. I don't think the guy ever sleeps. He's such a workaholic."

I snorted at that. "And you aren't?" I eyed the plethora of scars that disappeared under his collar. "Seems like you bring a lot of bounties in for the Academy." I winced as I said the last bit a little too harshly. Assuming he wasn't a moron, my tone only said one thing.

Bounties like me.

If he caught on that I didn't trust him, he didn't react to it. His utter confidence in bringing me to this Kaito guy made it clear that he felt like everything was going to be okay once I met him. I wasn't sure what to make of that, but I also was more curious to find out than scared about what might happen to me. If I felt like I was really in danger, then I had a trick up my sleeve even Dante wouldn't be prepared for.

I slipped my free hand into my pocket and turned over an artifact I'd stolen from Jess. She constantly pilfered magical charms from our supernatural guests when they were too busy ogling her breasts. She was so full of herself that she thought I wouldn't take one from her. It's not that I'd wanted to steal it, but I didn't trust Jess with anything more powerful than a toaster oven, so when I found out that she'd swiped a conjuring charm from a warlock studying the demonspawn, I knew I had to make sure to take it from her. She had no business being able to summon a demon from hell, and neither did I, frankly, but if I really needed to make a getaway plan then I was pretty sure summoning a real-life demon would throw any attackers off guard long enough for me to escape.

There was the minor issue about how to get back to Earth when I needed to, but I would tackle one problem at a time. For now, I was in a position of power and I'd be getting answers soon. It's not every day someone finds a back door to Fortune Academy.

"This way," Dante said and guided me up a winding row of wide stairs. Our footsteps echoed throughout the open space, bouncing off of marble and expensive mosaic tiles. I tried to imagine this place bustling with students all going to their next classes, bright and excited about their future. I didn't even know what kind of classes Fortune Academy offered.

"What's it like?" I asked, immediately hating myself for being so curious, but just the idea of going to school here had me intrigued. "Being a student at the Academy, I mean."

Dante grinned, his dimples returning and making him look a lot less intimidating. If it hadn't been for all his scars and his glowing eyes, he would almost look sweet when he smiled at me like that. "I graduated two years ago, so I can tell you that it's not easy." He nudged me with his shoulder. "But it's a blast."

That brought up one of the many questions I wanted to ask. What happened to a supernatural after graduation? "So, hunting was your calling?" I didn't know what I would want to do with my life. Right now I just wanted to figure it all out, who I was, why I was here, and why I couldn't remember anything. For the first time though, something more hinted behind a hunter's dimples. There could be a future for me here, if I could really become a student.

"Not quite," he admitted, "but it's what I'm good at." He turned down a corridor and we paused in front of a door with a single name label glimmering in silver at the top. *Kaito Nakamura, School Counselor.*

"Counselor?" I echoed the title, giving Dante a raised brow. "You're not bringing me to someone like, oh, I don't know, the Dean?" If anyone had enough money for a bounty hunter, it would be someone important, not a counselor. Wasn't that just a fancy name for a babysitter?

"Hell no," Dante said, leaning back as if horrified by the idea. "The last person you'd want to meet is the

Dean. She's fine on the surface but... well, let's just say that once you get to know her she's unreasonable and definitely would not welcome you here."

All the blood rushed from my face. For the first time since coming to the Academy my extremities tingled with cold. I gripped hard onto Dante's fingers, but I couldn't seem to extract his warmth from him like before. I ground my teeth in frustration. "Not welcome here?" I knew that Dante was selling me off as a bounty, but I'd assumed it was to become a student, not to sneak me in and sell me to some counselor. "Is that why we used a back door? I'm not even supposed to be here?"

My voice had gone shrill and Dante winced. He banged against the door. "Kaito! Hurry up! She's getting upset!"

I toyed with the idea of summoning the demon right here and now. If Dante thought he could just sell me to some lowly counselor then he had another thing coming.

The door swung open and the handsome Asian in a suit was not exactly what I'd been expecting. A single tattoo ran up the side of his left cheek, drawing my eye towards the streak of silver that followed his hairline. He definitely wasn't old. In fact he seemed to be maybe in his early twenties, a little too young perhaps to be a counselor, but there was such intelligence in his eyes that I didn't doubt for a moment that this was a man who was a force to be reckoned with. His gaze dropped to my hand that fumbled with the artifact in my pocket. All I had to do was crush it and I'd summon my distraction.

"Dante," the man said with an edge of warning to his voice, "you'd better back away from her."

Dante let go of me immediately and gave me space, which wasn't what I'd expected. None of this was making any sense. "Okay, you two better start talking or I'm going to get pissed off," I growled.

The man who I assumed was Kaito let his gaze linger on my pocket for another moment before he looked me in the eye. He didn't seem afraid, but he was determined. "I'm sorry if Dante frightened you, but when I learned of your existence and that you were with the Mother of Monsters I had to get you out of there." He ducked his head and swept into his office. "Please, come in. Have some tea."

Entering into a closed room with two men seemed like a bad idea, but the cozy space didn't look dangerous. A cheerful window lined with bonsai trees overlooked a courtyard and we were close enough to the ground that I could jump if I needed to. Plus, the tray of steaming tea just waiting for us did look inviting, and I was cold.

"Fine," I snapped and shoved past him. "But if you try anything—"

"You'll summon a demon to kill all of us," he

finished for me, smirking at my surprise. "You are safe here, Lily. I promise."

"Demon?" Dante asked, giving both of us a raised brow as he carefully edged around me and took the farthest seat.

No longer feeling the need to hide it, I pulled out the artifact and held out the soft bauble. The outside was translucent and contained a glowing red ember inside of it. It was hard, but delicate enough that I knew it would take minimal effort to crush it and release its magical energies. "Try anything and you'll wish you hadn't."

Dante cursed. "Sorry, bro. I didn't expect her to have an artifact. The girl doesn't even know what she is."

Kaito waved Dante's apology away as he poured us a cup of tea. "Important thing is that you got her here in one piece. Given the vision that Hendrik had, it's a miracle she's still alive."

"What vision? Who's Hendrik?" I asked.

Kaito placed the cup on the table in front of me and then backed away, making a point to give me space. "He's one of the mages here. He specializes in the dark arts and sometimes picks up glimpses of the future if they have a big enough impact to the timeline. He saw that you were supposed to die tonight."

I swallowed hard and then glowered at Dante. "Yeah, because a bounty hunter showed up at my place of work and spooked the people taking care of me." If Dante hadn't been there, it would have just been a night like any other, full of drinks, jokes, and watching Jess walk off with another date while I was left alone.

Kaito poured a cup of tea for Dante, but the hunter frowned at it. Sighing, the counselor placed the cup on the table and then poured one for himself. He took a leisurely sip before addressing me again. "If Dante hadn't been there, I fear there wouldn't have been anyone to stop what would have happened next." He looked at the artifact on my thigh. "You took that from someone, yes? I assume you had a good reason. What would have happened if that person found out you didn't trust them?"

I frowned and turned the bauble over in my hand before shoving it back in my pocket. I wrapped my fingers around the teacup and tried to draw from its warmth.

"What did you do?" Kaito asked.

I glanced up at him, but he was frowning at Dante. "I brought her," Dante growled. "What'd you want, me to pick up some human fast food while I was out too?"

Kaito didn't seem amused. "She's starving."

For some reason, I felt like he wasn't talking about food.

"I'm right here," I snapped. "I'm fine—" I tried to say, but my teacup rattled against its saucer as I started to shake. The cold had never gotten this bad before.

Kaito cursed and rushed to my side. I flinched, moving to get the artifact before he took it from me, but he placed both his hands on my face in such a gentle gesture that it startled me into compliance. I stared into his silver eyes, now that he was close enough I could see that they matched the streak in his hair. Beautiful.

"Lily, I need you to relax, okay? Your body is trying to protect itself but it doesn't have the reserves to perform magic. I need you to turn your defense mechanisms off."

Defense mechanisms? "I have no idea what you're talking about," I said, the words choppy as I convulsed from a new surge of cold that swept relentless needles through my body.

Kaito held out a hand. "Dante, give me your blade." When my eyes went wide, Kaito lowered his voice. "Lily, I need you to trust me right now. If you don't let me help you then you're going to die. If you break that summoning artifact in your pocket, then we all die. Even if I could teach you how to feed, I can't allow you to feed in the way your body needs, not here. That'll set off every alarm in this place and then we're all dead. You're just going to have to stay very still, can you do that for me?"

I was probably an idiot to trust this guy, but I was scared, and he felt like he knew what he was talking about.

Something about the cold running through my body wasn't normal. I had always pushed it off as a weird blood condition or that I just didn't retain body heat very well, but now that I was thinking about it, that was a pretty ridiculous notion. I knew that I was supernatural, so I should have listened to my body and picked up the cues. Something was wrong with me and even if I wasn't sure what it was, Kaito's experience said he'd seen this before and it didn't end well.

"Fine," I said and uncurled my fingers before placing my palms face-up on my thighs. "Do whatever you need to do."

Kaito nodded and then glanced at Dante who produced the same blade that he'd used to make our back door portal. Kaito swept two fingers over the steel and made it glow the same silver as his eyes.

I expected him to cut me with it, but he didn't. He let the cool kiss of the blade etch over my skin, leaving a sweeping rune to appear on my left inner forearm. He wiped over the skin once and seemed satisfied with the work before moving to my other arm and repeating the motion.

When he was done the sensation of ice filling my body subsided, except for the cool kiss of the runes across my arms. It was as if the magic had gathered all of the cold and pulled it into one place.

"That'll hold for now," Kaito said, wiping the sweat

from his brow. He returned the blade to Dante who frowned.

"You drained all of it. Hendrik's going to kill me."

I was starting to get curious about this Hendrik guy. If even Dante was afraid of him, then I wanted to know what kind of powers he had.

Kaito's gaze lingered on me for a moment and I blushed when I realized that he was eye-level with my breasts and had been staring for quite some time. He seemed to inwardly shake himself and gave me a nervous glance. I had the feeling that Kaito wasn't a guy who often got nervous. "I'm sorry about that, the runes, I mean," he added quickly. He rubbed the back of his neck before reclaiming his seat. He took a sip of his tea, but then grimaced and put it down.

"So what did you do, exactly?" I asked. I glanced down at my own cup and frowned at the layer of ice that frosted over it. Apparently I hadn't been imagining the intense cold that had been radiating through my body just a moment before.

"It has to do with what you are," he began, "but that's one question I'm afraid I'm not ready to answer for you yet. You need to ease into your truth, not be rushed and confronted by it. You've lost your memories, yes?"

I shifted uncomfortably in my seat and placed the frozen teacup back on the table. "What if I have?" I didn't like how much these guys seemed to know about me but I didn't know anything about them.

Kaito gave me a sympathetic smile. "That's okay. That's how most supernaturals come to us. When the Second Echo of Calamity struck and multiple realms collided, supernaturals were ripped from their homes and their lives. Such a traumatic event comes with a price."

"Are you saying I'm not from Earth?" I asked and crossed my arms. "That's quite the leap." I knew something was off about me, but I wouldn't go so far as to say that I didn't even belong on Earth.

Kaito shared a knowing look with Dante, making my irritation bristle. Dante cleared his throat before adding to the conversation. "We're not saying that you aren't from Earth, but well, let's just say that you're a complicated case."

"Then why am I not talking with the Dean right now? Why risk my life and bring me through a botched back door tunnel to the Academy? I'm sitting in an office with the two of you in the middle of the night and you're talking about me like I'm some secret."

"You are a secret," Dante said, his tone flat. "No one can know who or what you are."

I clawed my fingers into the seat, desperately wanting to shred something right now. "Even I don't know who or what I am!" That was the whole purpose I was here. If these guys weren't going to help then I was going to have to make them help.

"And it's best we keep it that way," Kaito agreed with Dante, his voice steady even though I was starting to get seriously pissed off. "Now that you're here, we can sneak you in with the new freshmen, get you a dorm and—"

"No," I snapped and shot to my feet, sending my shins hitting hard against the table and I winced. It was difficult to look intimidating when I was on the losing end of a battle with furniture. "I need to know what I am. How am I supposed to protect myself?"

"What do you need protection from?" Dante asked, crossing his arms while he managed to look insulted. "You can't seriously believe that I'd go through all the trouble to bring you here just to harm you. If I wanted you dead, then I would have done it at the bar and saved myself the trouble."

I pointed at Kaito who was still sitting all calm and reserved like we were in a regularly planned mentor-student meeting rather than whatever the hell this was. "You brought me to him to get your bounty. This is a school for supernaturals, right? You guys want to study me? I must be something special if both Fortune Academy and Monster Academy are fighting over me." I crossed my arms and tried to keep my pounding heart from flying out of my chest. Cindy and Jess, they'd done worse than just fight over me. They'd pretended to be my friends, my family, and the moment it looked like they weren't going to get their way, they were willing to kill me.

It hurt.

Kaito must have misunderstood the expressions I wore so carelessly on my face, because he sighed and opened his palms. I recognized the body language as a display of submission. He wanted me to feel like I was safe, but how could I ever feel safe again? How could I trust anyone not to just be looking out for themselves?

"I won't lie to you, Lily. Yes, the Academy studies the supernatural just as often as it takes on new students, but it's not a sentiment that Dante or I agree with. We work for the Academy, not the other way around, but this is where we can do some good for supernaturals like you. If you'll just give us a chance, I'll show you that this wasn't a bounty. You weren't collected to be studied, but if word got out who you were, then yes, that's exactly what would happen."

I swallowed hard. No matter how upset I was, or how betrayed I felt, I knew when someone was lying and Kaito was telling me the bold truth. This Academy wasn't perfect, he wasn't going to hide that from me, but if everything he was saying was true, he would be getting some major kudos from the Dean by turning me in now. It didn't make sense to hide me.

Feeling deflated, I plopped back onto the chair and

curled my fingers over my knees. I was glad I'd worn jeans today or else all my scrambling around through the realms would have skinned me pretty good. The fabric was streaked with dirt, blood, and rain. Getting myself a dorm and a hot shower was starting to sound pretty good right about now. "Okay, say that I go along with this. What's the plan?"

Kaito straightened and smiled, looking far too pleased with himself. "Orientation's tomorrow." He jumped up and rummaged through his desk, producing a badge with the school's emblem. He held it out to me. "Welcome to Fortune Academy."

BLACK AS NIGHT

I COULD TELL THAT KAITO WANTED TO GO WITH us, but Dante insisted that he take me to the dorms alone. With orientation in the morning the majority of the students would be preparing for the big day, either getting a good night's rest or doing the opposite, staying up and getting to know one another and making alliances.

"Unfortunately Fortune Academy is known for its cliques," Dante informed me, keeping his voice low as we moved through the streets lit by soft aura lights that matched a new color for every building. Dante said I'd get a color-code sheet in the morning for what each one meant. The colors would help me find which classes I needed to go to next and I needed to be careful wandering about because some buildings were reserved for specific magical power development courses. I didn't want to blunder into a class I wasn't ready for. "You'll have to find one where you fit in," Dante continued, "especially if you want to keep your head low. It's the outcasts that get the most attention." He gave me a once-over. "Have you displayed any supernatural powers yet, besides strength?"

A cool breeze played with my hair and I pushed the strands away as we walked at a leisurely pace. My fingers ran past the badge that Kaito had pinned on me and my touch lingered on the rough fabric. I was really here, but every instinct told me to run. I glanced up at the windows, unnerved to see the silhouettes of people inside when it felt like we should be in hiding. We'd entered the dorms and I didn't feel ready for this at all.

"I am not aware of any supernatural powers," I admitted. I hadn't even noticed strength being one of them until I'd resisted Dante's attempts to manhandle me. Was not taking any shit a superpower?

"Don't worry about it. They have programs for bringing out your powers." He winced. "Which, might not be a great idea. We can't have anyone finding out about the binding runes Kaito put on you." He glanced down at my arms and I turned my wrist over, noting that the mark had faded, but the cool sensation still kissed my skin. The bind was still there.

"So what are the cliques?" I asked, more trying to make conversation than anything else. I highly doubted

I'd fit into anything considered a clique. Being an outcast sounded pretty good to me.

"Most of the cliques are separated by supernatural species, but the Academy frowns on that, so they take in the oddball here and there to avoid getting separated." He held up his fingers and silently started counting off. "I don't know all of them, kind of out of the whole popularity contest bullshit since I graduated, but I can name a few. There are the Mages, the Mindfreaks, the Demis..."

I tuned out as Dante rattled off names that didn't mean much to me. Instead of trying to fit in with a group of supernaturals I hadn't even met, I was more interested in keeping to myself. Watching from the sidelines and learning was what I did best. I missed my cellphone, but this would be so much better than social media. I just had to keep my head down and not piss anybody off.

Should be easy, right?

DANTE SAID we needed to make a pitstop to talk with Hendrik first.

"The guy who spelled your dagger?" I asked, trying to keep my cool. "You sure you can trust him?"

"Hell no," Dante said without hesitation. "I don't trust Dark Mages any more than I do the monsters I hunt. They were classified as a branch of warlocks when the Academy was founded so the bastards weaseled their way into the Dean's good graces, but the students know better." He shrugged. "At least they're good at spells without asking too many questions." He squeezed my arm. "Hendrik doesn't know why you're here yet and we're going to keep it that way, all right? He saw you in a vision, but his visions are blurry and fast. The only way he'll recognize you is if you're up close, and even then he'll need some sort of confirmation. As long as you keep your distance, you'll be fine."

I nodded, partly relieved that I wasn't going to have to meet the Dark Mage, but at the same time apprehensive that Dante seemed like he'd broken so many rules to get me on school grounds without anyone knowing. How the hell was I going to get through tomorrow?

We paused at a building that glowed with ominous black aura lights, making the sleek exterior look cold and uninviting. I wrapped my fingers around my elbows and shivered, and not just because another uncharacteristically cool breeze swept over us. "I really don't want to go in there."

"Good, because you're not," Dante announced and placed his palm on the reader pad, initiating the doors to open.

"What?" I screeched and latched onto his arm. "You're just going to leave me out here by myself?" I glanced up at the building again, this time taking in the creepy gargoyles and statues that lined the pillars. "You can't be serious."

He peeled away my fingers and patted my hand. "I'll just be a few minutes. Hendrik needs to recharge this thing if I'm going to get you into the dorms, okay? We have a room set up for you, but we need to attune the pad to your magical signature. It's normally done during the registration process, but..."

"I'm not officially registered," I finished for him. "Fine. Go ahead, but if I get eaten by a gargoyle then you're to blame."

Dante grinned, making those delicious dimples reappear, and then he disappeared into the building's shadow, leaving me alone.

I didn't consider myself a patient person, and it was even worse knowing that I was in a strange place with no allies or friends. What if a Dark Mage came out of this building right now and demanded what I was doing here? What would I say? Oh, sorry dark magic dude, I'm just waiting for my bounty hunter to return with his dagger juiced up again so that he can take me back to the dorms. Yeah, that just sounded like a horrible pickup line.

Instead of waiting in the shadows to be picked off

the street by the next wandering Dark Mage, I took in a deep breath and leaned in closer to the touchpad. It hummed at my proximity, growing fainter when I crouched.

If the Academy asked for a blood sample as part of the application process, maybe that's because blood was what contained the magical signatures that secured this place. Testing out my theory, I pulled my shirt over my head, ignoring the cool air that snaked around my bare skin protected only by a flimsy bra, and rubbed the fabric on the bloodstains still soaked in my jeans. When I was satisfied enough of the red smear had transferred to the fabric, I held the shirt up to the pad.

Click.

The door slid open with a satisfying *whoosh* and I grinned. "That's right. Can't keep me waiting outside like some sort of pet."

Dipping inside before anyone saw me, I paused to gain my bearings. Only a few black aura lights illuminated the long entranceway and two spiral staircases that led upstairs. The creep-factor wasn't much better inside than it was outside, and it was even more freezing if that was possible.

My breath frosted in front of my face and I grimaced. Probably not the best idea to follow Dante into a building filled with Dark Mages, but it was a little too late to have second thoughts now.

I didn't want to reveal myself to Hendrik, but I did want to hear what he and Dante were talking about. Just because I'd trusted Kaito and Dante this far didn't mean that I was stupid. I stayed still and concentrated, trying to listen for any sign of life and grinned when Dante's low drones filtered through the air.

"Gotcha," I whispered, then scampered up the left staircase as quietly as I could. I felt like a right and proper ninja, until I reached the top step and fell flat on my face. "Oomph!"

I stayed on the ground and waited to see if anyone would come barreling out of the long corridor of doors, but no one seemed to have noticed my abrupt intrusion. I curled my fingers into velvet carpet and let out a sigh. "Okay, Lils, you can do this. Slow and steady."

I crawled along the carpet until I reached the source of the low murmurs. None of the other rooms showed signs of life, which I found odd given that this was apparently the Dark Mage dorms. They seemed like the type of supernaturals who'd stay up all night doing blood rituals or something creepy like that.

"What do you mean you used it up?" came an indignant reply on the other side of the door. I pressed my ear against it and held my breath as the sound of metal hit something solid as if someone had just thrown a knife against a hard surface, maybe marble or granite. These mages sure did live it up in these dorms. "I don't have unlimited magic, you know. Artifacts can hold a charge but it requires sacrifice, which, if you recall, is against Academy policy. What do you want me to do, cut off your hand and recharge it with your blood?"

Dante grunted. "If that's all it needed then I would have made sure to bleed on it instead of the street. Already had my hand cut off once today."

A moment of silence ensued and I tried not to roll my eyes. Dante really had to make himself sound so pompous, didn't he?

"I thought you said you were a hunter," the mage said, his voice dropping into low, threatening tones. "The only supernatural I know of that has that kind of healing ability is a vampire. I'm already in enough shit with the Dean. If she finds out I've been helping a fucking vamp—"

"Relax. I'm not a vampire. I'm just not your average hunter, okay? Now do what you need to do to recharge this thing."

"Why?" came the reply followed by a sliding sound as the dagger was picked back up again. "You clearly used a lot of magic already. What are you up to?"

Dante growled. "I came to you because you don't ask questions."

"Well that was before. Now you're coming back for seconds and I'm going to need a little bit more information."

"How about I cut you a deal," Dante said, lowering his voice enough that I almost couldn't hear him. I pressed harder against the door, wincing when the wood creaked. A moment of silence made me hold my breath while my heart thundered in my ears. I wasn't sure what I'd do if they found out I was eavesdropping on them. My mission right now was to get answers, not get myself into trouble, but sometimes those two things went hand in hand.

"I'm listening," the mage replied, making me relax with relief.

"I'll give you enough sacrifice to cover blood duty for a week. You'll be stocked up for a while, right? You won't have to go to your regular sources. The Dean is already giving the mages plenty of volunteers through the discipline program, but she's started to notice more people with injuries than are on the punishment docket. This'll help you lay low for a while."

A low hum of approval. "All right, hunter, you've got yourself a deal. I'll need some time to gather enough artifacts and then we can really test out your healing abilities. For now, show me your hand. That'll be enough to charge the dagger for you."

My blood went cold as I realized that Dante was going to lose his hand... again. And for what, for me? The second I heard his muffled cry my hand shot to the door handle, but I made myself freeze. I couldn't just bust in and yell at the Dark Mage. Dante had asked him to cut off his hand, even if that was dumb, a little piece of my frozen heart warmed.

He'd given a blood sacrifice... for me.

Tingling swept through my body and a magical hum sounded from the other side of the door. Dante's sacrifice had been made and now he was recharging the dagger.

I'd find a way to make this all up to him... somehow. Not sure what was worth two lost hands, but I'd figure it out. I didn't like to owe a debt to anyone. No matter his reasons, even if he was doing this for a selfish reason or for a longterm plan that I couldn't understand right now, he still was helping me when he didn't have to. In spite of myself, I was grateful.

"It's done," said the mage, making me scurry down the steps as fast as I could without being too loud.

I paused at the front door and frantically waved my bloodied shirt over the pad, but I must have smudged the blood on the floor when I'd fallen because it wouldn't pick up a signature.

"What do you think you're doing? I thought I told you to wait outside," Dante growled, although he sounded less menacing and more exhausted than anything else.

I peered at him over my shoulder and gave him and sidelong smile. "What can I say. It was creepy outside." I gave the ominous interior a once-over. While it was missing gargoyles like the exterior, faint runes fluttered over the walls as if spells were alive in the surface. If I focused, a faint whisper nagged at the back of my mind in a language I didn't understand. "It's not much better in here, to be honest."

He chuckled, then coughed and adjusted his arm deeper into the folds of his cloak. I narrowed my eyes on the evidence of what he'd just done. "How'd you even get in here?" he asked, then shook his head. "Never mind. I don't want to know. Let's get you to your dorms before anyone finds out we're here."

I wanted to prod him with questions about why he'd be willing to let a Dark Mage cut off his hand for me, and what other blood sacrifices he'd agreed to. Instead I followed silently as he activated the pad, this time by leaning down and looking into the screen. A small laser swept over his iris before the doors opened. So, it was more difficult to get out of the Dark Mage's dorms than in... that was interesting.

Once outside we passed by a few more buildings. One caught my interest, looking more like a stacked series of huts than the mix of modern and gothic archi-tecture on the rest of the campus. "What's that?" I asked, pointing to the tall pillars with buildings perched atop them.

"Panther shifters," Dante said absently, grunting and

failing to hide how much pain he was in as he stumbled. "They like heights... and walls they can chew on."

I rested a hand on his bicep and refused to pull away when he froze. "Dante, why did you need to recharge that dagger? And why aren't you healing?" I let my gaze fall meaningfully to the shadows in his cloak.

He rolled his shoulders back and straightened. "You weren't supposed to know about that. Don't ask too many questions, okay? That's how you're going to stay safe."

I frowned, but I wasn't going to push him. I didn't know enough about him yet to be sure if he was really trying to keep me safe, or if he just didn't want me to learn his secrets. He wasn't healing as fast as he had the first time, which either meant that his powers had limits, or whatever the Dark Mage had done to him had taken more than just his hand.

"Here we are," he said, indicating one of the larger buildings we'd come across. "This is the Freshman Ward. There's a room for you here until you figure out where you belong."

I looked longingly back at the other buildings, particularly the cool looking tree fort huts. "How do I know where I'm supposed to stay?" I didn't know if supernatural strength was a shifter trait, but being a panther sounded pretty cool, minus the chewing on the wood part, anyway.

He gave me a weak smile, his dimples reappearing for a delightful moment. "You'd be surprised how many freshmen don't know what they are or haven't shown signs of supernatural abilities yet. You'll fit right in once we get you on the roster. First step is attuning your blood to your room and the system will automatically log you, but it requires a spell, which is why I had to charge the dagger." He gestured at the large basin off to the side of the building that I'd mistaken for a broken water fountain. "You ready?"

Faint, pink and blue lights made the place look cute and inviting, but I couldn't shake the tingling sensation of warning that traveled up the back of my neck. If I registered my blood here, then there was really no going back. I'd be in the system illegally and if I was discovered as a fraud, I'd be expelled and never let back in.

"Couldn't I just apply like everyone else?" I asked and wrapped my arms around my chest. "What if this isn't a good idea?"

Dante held out his palm and waited for me to take his good hand. When I relented and slipped my fingers into his, he gave me a gentle squeeze. "This is the safest way for you to learn about your powers and master them. If you went through the normal registry then your blood would be tested and flagged. I need to override the system when we register you."

"Why would I be flagged?" I squeaked, starting to feel self-conscious.

Jess's words came back to me again.

You're a monster.

You're supposed to work for us.

What the hell kind of creature was I that my blood would trip a security alarm at a place like Fortune Academy? Why did Kaito have to bind my powers? What powers was he keeping in check that were so dangerous that he wouldn't even tell me what the hell I was?

"Hey, Lily. Stop freaking out on me."

I blinked a few times only to realize that Dante was leaning heavily against the fountain and looked like he was seriously ready to pass out. "Are you sure you're up for this?" I asked. He was right, I was freaking out, but if he passed out on me I'd freak out even more, and plus I felt kind of bad for him. Dark circles had formed under his eyes and he scrunched over as he tried to steady himself against the fountain, looking like he was on the losing end of an internal battle.

"Damn Dark Mage did something to me," he grumbled, then produced the stub of his hand. "Damn it, usually it's healed by now."

I tried not to pass out at the sight of blood and bone. The wound wasn't bleeding freely, but it looked more like a cauterized end where a hand should have been. "Do we need to get Kaito?" I offered, my voice wavering as queasiness settled over me. If the sight of gore made me uneasy, I hoped that meant at least I wasn't a vampire.

Dante chuckled. "Already looking up to him, are you? That's good. If you're ever in trouble then Kaito is the right guy to go to."

"I'm not looking up to anyone," I shot back. I didn't mean to sound defensive, but I was just trying to help. Kaito obviously had a good relationship with Dante. If anyone would know how to handle regeneration powers gone wrong it would be him—certainly not me.

"Yeah, okay," he said, chuckling as if he didn't believe me. "It's better for you if you learn to trust Kaito, but I get it. That'll come in time. I didn't trust anyone right away either and it saved my hide a few times."

Curiosity made me want to ask him questions, but Dante decided that pow-wow time was over. He positioned my wrist over the clear fountain and pulled out his blade. He whispered something I didn't understand and it glowed to life. An army could have descended on us and I wouldn't have noticed. The blade was gorgeous and its power called to me with warmth and enticement.

"Focus," Dante said, his words kind but stern. He awkwardly pushed my wrist to rest on the basin's edge with his elbow. It was hard to boss me around with one hand. "I'm going to cut you, okay? I need you to drop the blood into the basin and then stay very still."

Something in me panicked at the idea. Most people were used to cuts, but I'd been extremely careful in the bar with any potentially sharp object. For some reason the idea of cutting myself was terrifying. It was as if I had a limited supply of my blood and to lose any of it would be devastating, but I knew it was an illogical reaction. It had kept me from applying to Fortune Academy on my own, which apparently was a good thing. I would have triggered some bad mojo with them and never gotten the help I needed. I never would have met Kaito or Dante, and something told me that they had answers I needed, and perhaps I was more interested in them than I should be.

Dante rested the blade at the crook of my wrist and waited for my approval. I knew I had to say something to give him permission to cut me, which gave me a strange sense of power and relief. He wouldn't hurt me or do anything without my permission, at least for now.

"Do it."

Dante didn't hesitate and sliced across my skin. I expected it to hurt, but it was more like a cool breeze that swept across my wrist. I couldn't look down right away. Just the idea of seeing my own blood made me dizzy, or maybe that was already from the blood loss. Fuck, I was such a baby.

Dante flinched, then dunked his blade into the water and washed it with his cloak.

"What is it?" I asked. He seemed disturbed, but I was the one with a blood aversion issue. He was a badass hunter who chopped off his hands to pay debts to Dark Mages.

"I need to concentrate," he snapped, then closed his eyes and circled the blade in the water.

I knew I shouldn't have looked down, but curiosity won over.

What I saw confirmed any doubts I had that I was a monster.

My blood wasn't red... it was black.

NO PRESSURE

"WHAT THE FUCK, DANTE," I SAID, BREATHING in deep and slow so that I didn't pass out and drown myself in the basin of murky water. It had been clear a moment before, but now my blood—my very black blood—mixed into the waters and made it look like a swirling basin of shadows.

"Kaito warned me that might happen," he said. The way he kept his voice low and monotone was a tell. A guy like Dante didn't freak out, but when he got super calm, it meant that something was wrong. He continued to swirl the blade in the water and energy sparked from the handle. Dante flinched each time the snap of blue power struck him, but he didn't pull his weapon out. "It's just a side-effect of your heritage. Don't worry too much about it right now. I'm blocking the flag system so that it doesn't detect it."

I was so glad that this wasn't a public ceremony. Anyone with eyes would be able to see that something was clearly wrong with me.

You're a monster.

I bit my lower lip until tears formed in my eyes. This sucked so much. I wanted to be a cool supernatural, not something that was evil or deserved to be locked up in a place called Monster Academy. I didn't know what I was and now I wasn't so sure I wanted to know.

Yet, as Dante worked, I knew that uncovering who and what I was would be inevitable and it'd be a hard pill to swallow. Sweat formed at his brow and his fingers turned red with the heat of the magic coursing through the blade. It was taking a lot of power to keep the registry from picking up my monster blood.

"Is this going to work?" I asked, my voice more of a pathetic whisper than the measured tone I wanted it to be. "You can't rewrite my entry. If I'm a monster..."

"You're not a monster," Dante snapped, surprising me with the glow of his metallic orange eyes. They glowed brighter than I'd ever seen them as he worked with the Dark Mage's magic. "There's a part of you that's a rare supernatural, although even Kaito won't tell me what it is. I just know that there's a part of you that needs to be here and..." He trailed off and relaxed as the glow ebbed from the pool. "Doesn't matter. I was right.

The spell worked, look." He indicated the building behind me with a jerk of his chin.

I whirled to find the doors wide open and a glowing scroll of letters above it.

Welcome, Lily Fallen, Freshman of Fortune Academy.

MY EMOTIONS WERE SO frazzled that I didn't even ask, I just walked into the dorms and paused in the hallway. A few students glanced down at me, having gathered at the top of the stairs to loiter and talk.

"Who's the new girl?"

"They wander in sometimes. Slacker stragglers."

The rumors quieted when Dante followed me in and gave everyone a measured glare. Apparently having glowing eyes came in handy.

Dante brushed my arm with his fingers. The motion was natural as if we were already well-acquainted and strangely I found myself leaning into the touch. I told myself it was just because I was traumatized. I'd been betrayed by people I thought I could trust, discovered I bled black, but the reassuring news was that I wasn't completely a monster... just two-thirds of life-sucking evil. Based on the unforgiving glares of the students around me, that was a secret I'd better find a way to keep.

I didn't feel very evil, but guilt nagged at my chest anyway, as if I could control a heritage I couldn't even remember. I raised my chin high and tilted my head to Dante. "Well, you said I had a room? A girl gets tired, you know." And damn, was I tired.

He chuckled and rewarded me by slipping his arm around my waist. His fingers ghosted me, didn't quite touch me, but gave me a sensation of intimacy I didn't expect. He leaned in closer to my ear and his breath sent goosebumps down my neck. "They need to think I'm here to hit on you, so play along."

I fought the urge to frown. Right, there would be only two reasons why a bounty hunter would be with a blonde bimbo like me in the Freshman dorms. Either I was his bounty... or I was his booty-call.

Great.

I couldn't help but grate my teeth together every step we took as Dante guided me past curious stares. The students tried to pretend they weren't watching us with complete fascination. If they'd all just been recruited today, then this might be their first encounter with a hunter. Some of the more experienced students didn't seem fazed and whispered impolitely, no doubt informing the others what they thought was going on.

What Dante wanted them to see.

Even though this was a sham that would protect me, I didn't fucking like it one bit. My first day on campus and I was already going to get a reputation as the local whore? Not exactly the first impression I wanted to make.

My chest was getting tighter every step we took farther away from the entrance. "How far away is my room?" I complained. We'd already gone up three flights of stairs, past two corridors, and now I was in serious danger of being hopelessly lost in the maze of doors. I already had a terrible sense of direction and I wanted to be able to find my way out if I needed to.

"Here we are," Dante said and indicated the final door on the last row. "Trust me. You'll thank me for the placement."

I gave him a raised brow, then looked back at the door. The same kind of touchpad I'd seen at the mage dorms rested against the wall and I leaned down to look at it.

"No iris scanners here," Dante informed me. "Just put your hand up to it. It'll read your signature."

I scowled at him, then did as he said. The pad glimmered with a purple light and then a click sounded in the door. I opened the latch and a gust of cool air hit me followed by the stale scent of a room that hadn't been aired out in a while.

"Why do I get the feeling that this isn't a penthouse suite," I grumbled, then made my way inside.

My eyes adjusted to the darkness before Dante flipped a switch, revealing a room that clearly hadn't been used in quite a long time. Dusty sheets covered lumpy forms of furniture and a single window blocked any moonlight from coming in by an array of nailed up wooden boards. I lifted a lip at the drab scene.

"You really got me the best of the best," I drawled. "You shouldn't have."

Dante chuckled and ripped one of the sheets from a sofa. In spite of the plume of particles that launched into the air, the sofa itself looked quite comfortable. "No one will bother you here." He cocked his head to the side as if that was a lie. "Well, no one should bother you other than the other students. In any case, this is the safest place for you to be right now, I promise."

I scoffed and peeled away one of the sheets that covered a table which would take days to get clean enough to be fit for eating on. I sneezed at the new plume of dust kicked up by the disturbance. "Safe," I repeated the word, testing it for its validity. I wasn't sure if I would ever feel safe, at least not until I had all the answers that I was looking for and control over... whatever magic that ran through my veins.

My black veins.

I swallowed hard.

"The bathroom and showers are shared and at the other end of the hall, so I'd recommend going early in the morning if you'd like to avoid the rush," Dante continued, oblivious that my mouth was now hanging open.

"Excuse me, *shared*?"

He waved away my concerns. "These are the Freshman dorms, what'd you expect? You don't get special treatment just because you're at a prestigious academy." He grinned, his glowing eyes lighting up with mischief. "Follow the herd to orientation tomorrow. There will be an assessment involved to check your supernatural standing." His gaze dropped to my arms which were tucked securely around my chest. "I trust that Kaito's binds will hold. For the one-third that'll remain detectable from the test, I doubt you'll be able to be identified."

"What does that mean?" I asked, my voice squeaking into sonic realms. I didn't even care what Dante thought of me anymore. The whole idea of wandering around with a bunch of strangers into an assessment terrified the shit out of me.

He smirked and eased onto the sofa, dusting off the armchair. It didn't make sense that the covers hadn't done a better job keeping the furniture clean. "You know, you're the first bounty I've ever had that managed to cut my hand off—twice." He adjusted his injured arm that he still hid from me in the shadow of his cloak.

I edged closer to him and sat on the end of the sofa just within reach. "Well, if you're going to whine about it, then at least show me."

His gleaming eyes watched me. The effect of his gaze should have been unnerving, but I found him fascinating to look at. I always felt like eyes were the gateway to the soul, and if Dante's eyes glowed, then what a tasty soul he must have.

I flinched at the strange turn my thoughts had taken.

Did I just call his soul... tasty?

Dante surprised me by pulling out the stump of his arm where a hand should have been. "I'm afraid whatever Hendrik did to me might be permanent, and of course the bastard failed to mention that."

"A sacrifice is not truly a sacrifice without having lost," I said, my words barely a whisper as they came to me unbidden.

Dante hummed. "Insightful words, and likely true." He returned his arm into the folds of his cloak. "If you can do what Kaito hopes you can do, then you were worth the sacrifice, Lily."

My fingers dug into the dusty edges of the sofa. "And what is it that Kaito expects me to do?"

Dante's eyes flashed with violent promise. "Save us all."

MELINDA THE MUSE

Dᴀɴᴛᴇ ʟᴇғᴛ ᴍᴇ ᴛᴏ ᴍʏ ʀᴏᴏᴍ ᴀɴᴅ I ᴡᴀsɴ'ᴛ sure how I felt about that. His presence made me both anxious and excited, but now that he was gone, the reality of what I'd gotten myself into hit me like a wall.

No fucking pressure.

"Save us all, my ass," I grumbled as I ripped sheet after sheet off of more dusty furniture. The room was actually quite large with some expensive pieces in it. Once this place got cleaned up I was going to feel pretty fancy.

But man, this place needed a serious cleaning. I hadn't even noticed the chandelier cocked against the ceiling, tied up by a rope which seemed to be glued with a million cobwebs. There was a small kitchen with a sink filled with sandy grains that would be a nightmare to clean out. When I finally ventured into the bedroom I had to find the light switch. I ran my fingers across the walls—nothing. Just grimy, textured surface that made me want to go take a shower.

I'd always been good about seeing in the dark, but this bedroom had a haze over it that made it impossible to see anything. I needed at least some light to work with and if there was a window, I suspected it was nailed up tight with more wooden boards and nails.

Pain rocketed up my shin as I rammed into a piece of furniture. "Shit!" I cried and doubled over, only to fall onto a bed and land on a fur blanket. It was the first thing in the entire place that didn't smell like dust, so I breathed in and took a moment to recover.

"Well, at least I landed on something soft," I muttered.

I'm not soft, a voice growled in my head, sounding sleepy and not at all pleased at having been disturbed, *but you are pressing your breasts into my face, and those are kind of soft... and nice.*

I reeled back and slammed into the wall, my hand miraculously finding the light switch, sending a dull light to illuminate the room from the crackling bulbs.

A massive silver wolf stared back at me lazily, his eyelids drooping over crystal blue eyes. I hadn't landed on fur bedding... I'd landed on a wolf.

A wolf that could talk in my head.

"Niiiiiice wolfie," I said with a trembling voice as I

eased towards the doorway. "Didn't know... this room was occupied."

The wolf yawned, making me freeze as I stared at sharp canines. He stood and shook himself, sending fur flying to join the floating dust motes that hung in the air. *I'm not a wolfie,* the voice said again, this time sounding more irritated, *I'm just a wolf. I can shift back if it would make you feel better, but I didn't bring a change of clothes.*

"Uh, what?" I asked, adrenaline making my fingers go numb. Or perhaps that was that thing that always happened to me when I needed to touch someone or else I'd freeze to death. Shit. Now was not a good time to need to recharge.

The wolf glowered at me some more before the unmistakable sounds of bones crunching filled the room. I stared in mortified horror as the wolf shifted before me, his long canine front legs changing into muscular arms as he unfurled to stand upright. Fur retreated into smooth, supple skin and his snout retracted to reveal a gorgeously handsome face. His fangs didn't retreat all the way, leaving a sinister look about him along with the piercing intensity of blue eyes that watched me with the steadiness of a predator. Then he lifted his lip in a snarl and had the audacity to look at me like I was the intruder. "How did you get in here?" he asked, narrowing his eyes at me.

So, he was a shifter... and very naked.

I propped my hands on my hips and tried to look threatening while keeping my chin high. Even though he'd just revealed himself to be a dangerous supernatural, I got the sense that he was all bark and no bite. Floppy hair fell into his eyes that were already starting to droop and he stifled a yawn while he waited for me to reply.

"I'm a new student," I said, keeping my tone steady. I was sore, tired, and didn't have time for this shit. "This is my bedroom," I clarified, "and if you hadn't noticed, this is the girls' freshman dormitory. I think you are the intruder here."

The shifter rolled his shoulders back, making his chest more prominent. It was a challenge not to let my eyes dip to the even more impressive package he boasted.

As if he sensed my hesitation, his gaze slowly swept over me and deliberately lingered on my breasts that had apparently just been in his face a moment ago. I blushed when his cock hardened just by looking at me. His eyes flashed up to mine again and a grin quirked at the side of his mouth. "Well, if you'd like to stay, perhaps I'm up for that."

I did not like the gleam in his eye. I bared my teeth at him, assuming it would be an appropriate response in this situation. "I don't want to have sex with you," I said.

His eyebrows shot up. "Who said anything about sex?"

I pointed at his cock that was fully erect now. "You are."

He shrugged as if he stood naked and aroused in womens' bedrooms all the time. "Sorry, it's a natural reflex. You're the one who put your breasts in my face." He grinned again, his gaze dipping, as his tongue swept over his lips. "Can't blame me for having primal instincts. It's in my blood."

I snapped my fingers to get his attention away from my breasts which seemed to enjoy his gaze a bit too much. "Hey, up here buddy. I don't care about your primal... needs. I care about what I need. I need to get settled in, take a shower, and then get some sleep before orientation tomorrow. That means you need to get the fuck out of my room."

He held up both hands in mock defense. "Whoa, whoa. Don't need to get so defensive." I growled, which apparently he thought was hilarious because he barked a laugh, making his hips jut out and his cock bounce out with them. Did he have no modesty whatsoever? "I could help you with some of those things, but, if you don't want me in the way then I will just sleep on the other bed. You won't even know I'm here." I balked at him and he winked at me. "I like it here. It's quiet and no one bothers me, at least until now. But baby, you're stunning and funny, so I'll allow you to bother me anytime."

I rolled my eyes and was about to tell him off when

he flinched and the unmistakable sound of a bone cracking made me wince. He buckled over and opened his mouth on a silent cry as the shift took hold. The process looked painful, unnatural, but he bore down on the agony as if he'd done it a million times before. At least the shift was quick, and then he was that beautiful silver wolf looking at me again.

He stretched out and leaned back, his front paws curling into the carpet as he yawned, pain and bone-breaking already forgotten. He shook himself before he pranced over to the second bed near the wall and jumped up on it. Making a little circle, which I had to admit was adorable, he settled down into a pile of messy blankets and fur.

"You are seriously not sleeping here," I insisted.

He opened one blue eye to regard me, then closed it again. I got the sense that I could try to move him... but it wouldn't end well for me.

With a huff I decided to ignore the creature and rummaged through the bedroom's dresser. There were clothes and they actually didn't seem too dusty. I held up a pair of cotton pants that looked like they'd fit me and then plucked out a t-shirt. I glanced at the wolf when I was done, finding his breaths were now coming long and shallow. I found it particularly insulting that he could fall asleep just like that with a stranger in the room.

My room.

I'd talk to Dante in the morning about the wolf intruder... for now, I just wanted the basics. Shower, maybe a snack, then sleep. Sounded like heaven to me.

I HADN'T FOUND anything to eat, but it was late enough that I could just tell my stomach I'd fill it with something in the morning. The showers were down at the end of the hall. Going late at night was apparently a bad idea since a bunch of girls in towels were hanging out getting absolutely nothing done other than jabbering with one another.

I kept my head down, but it didn't stop the onslaught.

"Hey, it's the girl who's screwing the hunter. He gone already?" She plucked at my jeans, rubbing the dried blood on her fingertips. "He never takes *me* on his hunts. I'm going to have to have a word with him."

Jerking my head up to stare at the girl, I found someone who reminded me of Jess. Curves that could kill and a devilish gleam in her eyes made her look like a succubus, but I knew that supernaturals that fed off of life-force couldn't be recruited at Fortune Academy, still, I wasn't sure how solid the rules were. I was here, after all, so I decided to play it safe. "He left," I confirmed, then ducked my head again and prowled past her. I was here to get a shower, not feed the local gossip.

"Hey, where you going?" she asked with a screech to her voice and clawed out at my arm.

I stiffened when foreign energy filtered over my skin, but I shrugged it off and kept walking.

"Did you see that?" her friend whispered. "Pushed away a muse's compulsion like it was nothing. What the fuck is she?"

A muse had tried to push compulsion on me? I didn't even know what a muse was, but if she'd just tried to make me do something against my will, then she had another thing coming.

I knew I should have just kept walking, but something in me snapped. No one messed with free will, especially mine. "Who the fuck do you think you are?" I growled, my fingers curling into fists. I'd had a long, rough ass day and this bitch wasn't helping.

She blinked her bright eyes at me with pure innocence. "Oh, my dear. I'm sure you don't want to talk to me that way. You've only just arrived and I'll cut you some slack for that." She grinned. "I'm Melinda and you'll learn there's a hierarchy around here. I'm a muse, which puts me in the top supernatural category." She leaned in and poked me in the chest with a sharp fingernail. "You, whatever you are, can't possibly beat that.

You'll do well to stay out of my way. You've already caused enough problems."

Not sure what problems I had caused. The bitch had gotten in my face, not the other way around.

"And stolen one of the hottest guys," grumbled her friend.

Yeah, Dante was hot, but he wouldn't touch these girls with a nine-foot-pole. Somehow I just knew he wouldn't be into snooty bitches no matter how gorgeous they were and I decided I liked him even more for that fact.

A small crowd had formed around us and tension cut the air. Now that I got a better look at the girls I shared the dormitory with, I noticed they were all drop-dead gorgeous. If the girls were this hot... I wasn't even sure if I wanted to meet the guys. Based on my experience so far with Dante, Kaito, and the wolf shifter, supernaturals had an affinity for good looks.

"Look," I said, dropping my voice and turning my body to the side, hoping that the gesture came off as non-threatening, "I've had a long day. If you want to go for Dante, then I'm not going to stand in your way. Really."

The muse narrowed her eyes at me and she crossed her arms, her breasts plumping underneath her towel with the movement. "I'll figure out what you are tomorrow at orientation," she said and I got the sense that her words were supposed to be a threat. "Until then, I'm not going to waste energy on you, so have a nice night." She turned on her heel and her friend's eyes widened before scampering after her.

With a sigh I glared at the crowd until it dispersed, leaving me alone. I stalked into the showers, found a box with travel-size toiletries and helped myself.

By the time I towel-dried my hair, got into my dusty PJs, and made it back to my room without incident, I was exhausted. For some reason thwarting whatever compulsive magic Melinda had tried to use on me had worn me out. I felt the lingering tingling of what she'd tried to do to me.

Come orientation, I certainly hoped I could figure out what I was so that I'd have a better chance to survive this place before I got the hell out.

As long as I didn't bleed... I should be okay.

The wolf rested motionless in the nearby bed, but I was too exhausted to care. If he wanted to maul me in my sleep, let him try. I still had the conjuring artifact, then panicked when I realized that I'd left it in my pants pocket. I rummaged through my dirtied clothes and plucked out the translucent orb. It swirled with a deep ruby red energy and made me feel queasy to look at it too long, but it was functional.

My pajamas didn't have pockets, so I tucked the orb underneath my pillow. I used two pillows to make sure I wouldn't accidentally crush the orb in my sleep and unleash hell in the middle of the night, but if I needed it then it would be there.

I left the main light on. It didn't seem to bother the wolf and had been on the whole time I'd been in the showers, so I decided I'd rather not sleep in the dark tonight.

Closing my eyes and finding darkness in my mind, I drifted off into a restless sleep with only the sounds of a wolf's soft snoring to keep me company.

ORIENTATION

THE NEXT MORNING I WOKE UP AND HAD already forgotten where I was. An instant of panic set in as I frantically looked around the room, only to have everything from the night before came rushing back to me. I glanced at the bed, but aside from tousled sheets and loose fur, there was no wolf to be found. Guess he'd gone back to his own dorm come sunrise.

I wasn't sure how he'd gotten out, since the bedroom had only one window and it was boarded up, but then I noticed the small chewed out hole and rolled my eyes. A thick black sheet laid out folded neatly on the floor which must have been what he'd used to cover up the hole to keep it pitch black in here. Yet, he'd let me sleep with the light on and hadn't turned it off when I'd gone to take a shower. Maybe he was trying to show me that he could be trusted.

Whatever the wolf's motivations, the image of his perfect body and even more perfect cock flashed through my mind. I pinched myself as punishment. "No sex with wolves," I reminded myself. "No sex with anyone here." The last thing I needed was to make myself vulnerable or build attachments with dangerous supernaturals I didn't yet understand. I didn't even know if I was a virgin or not—one of the many downsides to having lost my memory of who I was before Cindy's bar. I needed to focus on myself before I did anything like that, even if my body disagreed with me.

I was used to feeling cold, but the thought of the wolf shifter's plain advances made me shiver. Then I remembered I would get to see Dante again today and another shiver went through my body, sending unforgiving heat to my core.

Fuck, I needed to get laid.

An annoying cascade of laughter poorly muffled by the wall reminded me that I needed to "follow the herd" as Dante had said it. I didn't know where orientation was and I doubted he would come to guide me personally. Everyone would be out on the streets by now and I wasn't interested in drawing any more attention to myself than I already had. Walking around with a hunter hadn't done me any favors so far with the local students.

I got ready as fast as I could and found a uniform to wear that fit me, although a bit too snugly for my taste. I was too tall for most things I tried to wear and I didn't have a mirror to check myself out, but I felt like I was showing off a little too much thigh. Whatever. I was sure the dress code around here would be flimsy at best given the show the wolf shifter had given me last night. I found my demon conjuring artifact still snuggled under my pillow, so I plucked it out and put it in one of the skirt pockets. If I had to wear a skirt... at least it had a practical side to it.

I combed out my hair with a brush I'd procured from the toiletry bin in the showers and even found some makeup, although I didn't bother to put any on. Jess had always fussed at me that makeup existed to be used, but I hated the stuff.

My heart twisted thinking about Jess.

Taking a deep breath, I opened the door and inspected the gaggle of girls swarming like hornets around their queen. There was Melinda all dolled up with her gorgeous black hair unfurling in voluptuous waves over her shoulders. She cast me a venomous glare as if daring me to approach.

I mean, it was a one-way hall to the rest of the dormitory and there was only one exit that I knew of, so Melinda the Muse was just going to have to fucking deal.

Holding my chin high, I marched down the hall. The group grew quiet as I approached. By the time I reached them, I wasn't sure what to do next. I knew I had to go down three flights of stairs, but my sense of direction was horrible to say the least.

"We'll be keeping an eye on you," Melinda said, her sneer flashing before she smiled sweetly and then stalked off, her entourage in tow.

I wondered what the other girls were who followed her out. They all looked like a normal group of university students with tight-fitting uniforms that put my own modesty concerns to shame, hair up in ponytails or down loose around their shoulders, and each of them had a tiny notebook in hand. I frowned. Dante never mentioned a notebook.

Keeping my distance, I followed the girls outside and took in the Academy in the broad light of day, or at least what passed for day in a place that was clearly not Earth. A soft glow overtook the campus like a pseudo-sunrise, but I couldn't spot a source. It felt like the sky was a hazy orb, kind of like we were inside of my conjuring artifact, and it made me feel uneasy.

Shaking my head, I followed the girls down the street before I lost them. The last thing I wanted to do was wander around the Academy grounds with no idea where I was going. I probably could find Kaito's office if I tried, maybe, I think.

It was hard not to get distracted. Students were everywhere and none of them were shy about their supernatural powers. A pack of wolves startled me as they ran by, giving chase to a single panther. Eyes wide, I watched the group rampage down the streets. No one was screaming for their lives or even gave the predators much of a second glance.

When the panther tried to double-back and dive through a group of what I guessed to be witches based on their black uniforms, the girls sneered at the rowdy shifters that were barreling straight for them. One witch whispered and magic glowed across her hand, sending a forcefield around her and her friends to deflect the creatures who pinged off of the shield in continued pursuit of their lost prey.

"So we meet again," a male voice caressed me from behind, hot breath on my neck.

I whirled to find the wolf shifter from the night before in front of me again. Of course, he was still naked.

I glanced over his body involuntarily, taking in his prominent thighs and muscular chest. I knew I should probably be offended, or at least embarrassed that a naked man was standing in front of me, but I couldn't help but admire him and the ease with which he carried himself.

"Like what you see?" he asked, lowering his voice and taking a step closer to me.

I snapped my gaze up to his gorgeous face, taking in the hard line of his jaw that looked... kissable. I shook myself. *Focus, Lils.* "I'm heading to orientation," I blurted, then my stomach dropped when I realized I'd forgotten to keep an eye on Melinda. I shoved the shifter aside, painfully aware of his hard bicep under my fingers, as I searched for my own prey. "Damn!" I hissed. "You made me lose her. Now I don't know where to go."

"I can show you the way," he said cheerfully.

Turning to face him again, I glowered. "Aren't you too busy chasing pussy cats?" I regretted it the moment I said it.

His grin turned absolutely sinful. "What if I'm chasing pussy right now?"

I rolled my eyes. "Then you're in for a disappointment," I promised, even though heat was already throbbing in some very private places. I didn't understand why this shifter was getting under my skin. I wasn't one to drool over a guy.

He shrugged. "Can't be disappointed when I just like being around you." He winked. "I'm Logan, by the way."

I crossed my arms. "Is that why you refused to leave my bedroom all night?"

He smirked. "I was there before you were. Called dibs."

"You can't call dibs on a girl's bedroom!" I shrieked, but my protest fell on deaf ears.

Logan transformed back into his wolf in record time. I wondered if it hurt as much as it seemed it did. The idiot shouldn't shift just so he could talk to me. He'd pushed his voice into my mind the first time I'd met him, so I knew he could still communicate. He was just being stubborn.

I made a mental note to yell at him about being a dumbass later.

Or... maybe he just wanted to show off his dick again. Yeah, that sounded like a good enough reason to go through an agonizing shift that broke every bone in his body to a guy like Logan.

With a sigh, I followed the wolf that was now whining at me. He was quite cute in his wolf form and it wasn't hard to spot him winding through the sea of legs. I hoped that he was guiding me to the right place, but I didn't have much choice in the matter. If he led me out of the crowds then I would stop following him, but for now I felt safe enough surrounded by other students that Logan wouldn't try anything.

I quirked a smile at the thought that a crowd of supernaturals actually made me feel safe. Maybe this place wouldn't be so bad after all.

It took me a while to realize that the campus was laid out in a large series of overlapping circles. The path

Logan was taking me on cut straight down the middle of an endless row of buildings. The various colored torches shone as brightly in the day as they had at night indicating a type for each building and I was looking forward to getting to learn my way around this place. I couldn't rely on a wolf guide to get me to my next class every time.

The epicenter of Fortune Academy took my breath away with a massive spire that looked like it could have been a part of Maleficent's Castle. It was gorgeous, as if the entire building had been carved in a single night by a jeweler out of onyx. I spotted Melinda and her crew at the entrance. She gave me a healthy glare before gliding inside.

It felt good to piss her off and I smiled, feeling almost giddy, and looked around for Logan to say thanks. Various students in crisp uniforms wandered through the heavy traffic center and I couldn't spot him. If he'd stuck around, then it would be easy for a silver wolf to get lost in the crowd.

I shrugged it off, deciding that Logan had gone back to his pack now that I was safely at my orientation, and I took the long, grand steps into Fortune Academy's Center Hall.

The interior was just as impressive as the exterior complete with embossed engravings of various supernatural icons on the walls. I figured I should probably recognize them, but I didn't. Maybe my classes would include supernatural history. There was one engraving that drew my attention and I wandered to it, feeling drawn like a moth to a flame.

A statue of a beautiful woman with a golden crown atop her head caught my attention. Even through the hard onyx stone the golden glow came through as if gold dust had been sprinkled into the carving along with little pieces of the sun. She stood tall and proud, boasting a single red necklace with a magical glow of its own that felt oddly... familiar.

"I see you've found Sonya, the Queen of Hell," said a voice that had me whirling.

Dante gazed down at me with his enticing orange eyes, as if the gods had crafted him out of amber and set his irises aflame. "Queen of Hell?" I murmured, trying to focus. Shit, what was it with the guys around this place? I scratched at the invisible spot where Kaito had placed binding runes on my arms. I wondered if they were having an adverse effect on me.

Dante smiled and he looked over my head at the magnificent carving. "Orientation will go over some of this, but this room shows all the Academy's founders and supporters. Even though it breaks all sorts of rules, Sonya comes to visit now and again. She's the Queen of Hell, but before that she was a vampire, and before that she was a succubus.

I quirked an eyebrow. "She sounds like she's been busy."

He chuckled. "Yeah, you could say that. In any case, I'm glad you found the Center Hall. Are you ready to go? Orientation will start soon and we can't have you being late." He offered his arm, then grimaced when he realized he'd pulled the stub of his amputated hand out of the folds of his cloak.

Choosing to walk stoically together, I stuffed my hands in my skirt pockets, feeling comforted when my touch ran across my conjuring stone. Dante was being friendly enough, but he'd still left me to fend for myself. "Is there a reason you couldn't have picked me up this morning at the dorms?" I asked, trying not to sound like a scorned ex-girlfriend and failing. "The girls and I really don't get along and I had to follow a wolf to this place."

He chuckled. "I didn't expect you to make friends with those girls." He gave me a nudge with his elbow. "They're competitive and petty. Even if you aren't displaying your powers yet, a supernatural worth her blood can smell your power from a mile away."

I tucked my chin against my chest. "Oh," I murmured. I'd hoped to keep a low profile, but apparently supernaturals could... smell me. "I thought Kaito's binds were supposed to help with that?"

He glanced around at the crowd, but no one was paying attention to us.

Right, *secret* binds.

"Sorry," I grumbled, then growled. "I just had a rough night. Did you know that the wolf shifter I mentioned slept in my room all night? He wouldn't leave! Is there anything you can do about him?"

Dante surprised me by laughing. "It shouldn't surprise you that a wolf decided to court you. Like I said, you smell incredible."

I stopped in my tracks. "You said I smell. You never said that I smelled... incredible."

A blush ran up his neck and he adjusted his cowl as he cleared his throat. "Well, I wouldn't worry about it, the wolf, that is. If he's courting you, then that'll help your adjustment into Fortune Academy with the other students. If you decided to tolerate his attention, his pack will accept you and also protect you."

While I liked the idea of having an army of wolves to set on Melinda, I didn't like the idea of selling my body to one of their pack to build an alliance. "I'm really not that kind of girl," I began, even though just being close to Dante made me want to run my fingers underneath his cloak and suck out his warmth like I had done just the day before. Gods, something was definitely wrong with me.

Dante chuckled. "Wolves aren't like that. Sure, they're primal and passionate, but if he's really courting you, then he's just testing his boundaries. The relationship doesn't have to progress any further than you want it to and you can still form that alliance." He smirked. "It's not like you're going to marry him."

I couldn't believe that Dante was encouraging me to date a wolf.

I narrowed my eyes. "You sure you won't get jealous?" I asked, daring myself to test the waters with him. I felt like the hunter and I had come to an understanding with one another and he'd shown that I could trust him to some extent, at least for now. So far everything he'd told me had come true. I wasn't sitting in a dungeon somewhere getting magically poked and prodded, although, I had a feeling that was coming next. It wouldn't be anything that the other students weren't already going through, so it would be on my terms. At least, I hoped so.

He surprised me by taking my hand, which was awkward since he had to reach around with his one remaining good hand. "You bet your ass I'll be jealous, but I'll get over it." When my eyes went wide, he tugged me closer to him and wrapped his arm around my shoulder. He leaned in close and I held my breath, wondering what he was going to say next. "You're clever. If we keep up the pretense that I'm interested in you, then that'll give me a good excuse to help you around the Academy and keep an eye on you."

I swallowed hard. I hadn't intended it to be a facade.

I genuinely wanted to know if he was interested in me. He'd already invested so much time and energy into getting me settled and what did he get out of it? If he wasn't interested in me... then he was getting something else, and I intended to find out what it was.

If Dante wasn't interested in me, he made a good show of faking it. He smiled and kept me against his hard chest, his hard jawline looking irresistibly kissable up this close.

I mentally shook myself as we ventured deeper into the Academy's Central Hall. I'd figure out what was going on. Maybe when I saw Kaito again I could learn more about the binds he'd put on me and if it could explain my... growing appetites.

I shrugged off the fear that I was a succubus and my powers were just now manifesting. There were worse monsters I could be, I supposed, but I wanted to be attracted to someone because of a genuine connection, not because something in me needed to feed.

The grand halls all ran together at the epicenter of the Central Hall, leaving me gaping up at a semi-circle of massive doors propped open. Inside was a room that seemed to have no ceiling and when we stepped through the entranceway, I gaped up with shameless awe.

"Wow," I murmured, taking in the column spires that traveled all the way to a pinnacle at the ceiling's skylight. "This place is incredible."

Dante followed my gaze, looking up and admiring the view for himself. Then he brought my attention back down to the crowded chamber. "We have a large influx of students today. It's good timing." He removed the warmth of his arm from my shoulder and nudged me by placing his hand on the small of my back. I hated the shiver that induced from me. "You'll be able to blend in, but not if I keep hanging around you. I trust you can manage the rest of orientation on your own?"

I glared at him. Like I had really needed his help to get from the entrance to the center of the building. He had alternative motives to come talk to me and I didn't like that he wasn't just being straightforward with me. "I'd like to see Kaito again later," I said, my words cutting harsher than I intended.

He nodded. "That can be arranged. Once you're through orientation and have your class schedule, it'll be excuse enough to see him. You'll be assigned a guidance counselor, since Kaito is a bit higher rank, but you can invent a problem and request to see him, then it'll all be legit."

As much as I wanted to see Kaito sooner rather than later, Dante had a good point. I was trying *not* to draw attention to myself, so I'd do things his way for now and play along. "Fine," I said and turned from him. I wanted to ask when I'd see him again, but I had a feeling he'd reappear whenever he felt like it and otherwise I would be on my own.

Don't get too attached, Lils, I told myself.

I was here with a purpose. I was going to find out who and what I was, and then I was going to figure out how to protect myself from Monster Academy. I wouldn't be able to hide forever and when they eventually found me, I'd be ready for them.

In spite of my resolve, I found myself peeking over my shoulder to see if Dante was still there.

He wasn't.

DON'T BE A DUD

"Everyone please find a seat," came a soft but authoritative female voice. I looked around the room for speakers to explain how clearly I'd just heard that voice, but didn't see any.

Then I spotted the source. Every eye in the room went to the beautiful woman who glided up the steps to the top of the center stage. Her silver hair was so striking that it might as well have been a diamond crown atop her head. Her glistening blue eyes swept over the gathering as she put on a fond smile that made even my heart warm. She came off as genuine, caring... and powerful.

Her words crashed over us with a wave of what I realized was magic... raw magic.

"Some of you may already know me," she said, spinning us all into a spell with that smile again and I tried to remember where I'd seen her before, "but for those of you who don't, I am the Dean."

Whoa, that was the Dean?

Then I remembered. Guinevere Lancelot. I'd thought the name was a joke, but that was the Dean. She was an ancient immortal and she had a short bio page on Fortune Academy's website about her history of clashing with humanity and her mission to bring supernaturals safely into the human world. After the Second Echo of Calamity and the merging of supernatural realms with Earth, there wasn't much sense in hiding the supernatural realm from humanity anymore. She'd been just as genuine and kind in her bio as she was now, although the image online hadn't nearly done her justice.

"When we speak in person, you may call me Gwen." She grinned and scanned the room. Briefly, her gaze caught mine and every muscle in my body froze as she took a moment to make every student feel the force of her presence. I wondered if it was magic that made it feel like she was talking directly to me and not to anyone else. "Today's orientation is to be led by none other than our prized professor Merlin. He's been a mentor and guide to me as long as I've been alive,"—she covered her mouth to poorly hide a chuckle—"which I will admit has been a long time."

A low murmur of approving laughter rolled through the auditorium and I cleared my throat hesitantly. I spotted a white-haired professor behind her in a navy blue suit, although if he was Merlin, he didn't look a day over thirty. I guessed that if Guinevere and Merlin were really immortal supernaturals, they wouldn't age.

She pointed to the end of the hall and the crowd turned to follow. "This Academy was founded by Evelyn, Queen of the Royal Covens, and Renee, Keymaster and Fate Witch." Two looming statues stood over us. The marble made their eyes look like they glowed. It was easy to pick out which one was Evelyn. The statue was impeccably carved, displaying fine dark lace that covered her body and a neat little crown atop her head that glistened with multiple gems, each representing a different witch coven. The woman beside her, Renee, held a staff in one hand and a deck of cards in the other. "If you are capable enough to find yourself among the graduating class, you will get a personal sendoff by the founders," Gwen added, leaving a ripple of excitement to pass through the crowd.

I was trying not to get caught up in the hype of being a member of Fortune Academy given my very illegal admission, however I couldn't help but picture myself among the graduating class getting to talk with such powerful supernaturals. If I could prove to myself that I wasn't a danger and could be helpful, maybe I did have a place here.

It was wishful thinking.

"Are you buying this?" a low male voice asked and I flinched to find Logan standing next to me. I hadn't seen him with clothes on before, not that his sloppy uniform could be called clothes. He wore a blazer without an undershirt and a tie dangled from his neck. The long stretch of fabric gave my eyes a guide to follow down the hard lines of his naked chest to the loose waistband that hung precariously low around his hips. When he chuckled, I snapped my eyes up to his and glowered.

"Why are you bothering me?" I whisper-yelled. I hadn't had enough time to make a decision regarding Logan and his wolf friends. I figured if I made alliances they would be hard to undo and what enemies did the wolves have? Other than... chasing giant cats around campus.

He jerked his chin, indicating a glowering Melinda I hadn't noticed until now. "Muse bitch has been trying to compel you the entire speech and she's getting pissed off that it's not working."

Startled, I glanced at her, and indeed the bitch was shooting dagger glares at me. "How do you know she's trying to compel me?" I asked, lowering my voice.

He glanced behind us. "Looks like you deflected the compulsion and... well, look."

I'd been so engrossed with Gwen's speech which I was now missing that I hadn't even noticed the growing pile of bodies behind me. A group of girls had curled up into the fetal position and fallen asleep right in the middle of the floor, many of them sucking their thumbs."

Was that my fault?

I glared back at Melinda who flipped me off and turned her attention back to the speech as if she hadn't just wiped out a pile of students with compulsive magic to regress into a baby state.

Having been introduced during my silent exchange with Melinda, Merlin took the stage. He gave a fond smile to Gwen, then braced himself on the podium and surveyed the crowd. He frowned at the litter of passed out bodies, but glossed over it as if supernatural pranks were to be expected even on orientation day.

"Today is the most important day of your lives," he began, his voice booming like Gwen's had over us, but with less subtle fondness. He took a moment to glare at Melinda who curled in on herself. A wave of smugness swept over me. At least he'd noticed. "Today you accept your role and responsibility as a supernatural," he said, giving her a moment of his attention before he addressed the group, "even if you don't know what that all means quite yet." His gaze seemed to fall on me and I cast my gaze to my feet until he continued. "We will start by having you break off into teams. Those of you who have already formed alliances please keep within your estab-lished groups of three or more. A maximum of ten is allowed for this exercise. We will proceed with the place-ment ceremony, after which you will be assigned your counselor and class schedule." He waved his hands in dismissal. "Let's begin!"

Logan grabbed my hand before I had a chance to see what everyone was going to do. "You're with me!" he announced with a bark to his voice, making him sound like an excited puppy.

"Wait!" I cried, but Logan yanked me hard and we dove through the crowd.

He dragged me through clamoring bodies as the students paired off into groups. I spotted the silver crown of Gwen's hair as she made her way across the stage and waved her hand, forming a basin out of thin air like the one in front of my dormitory. A shiver ran through me. I hoped that this assessment wouldn't require blood or else my cover would be blown before I even had a chance to take my first class.

I reminded myself that Dante and Kaito had set this all up so that I could join orientation as an official student. They wouldn't have gone through all that trouble to keep me a secret unless they knew what the assessment entailed, so I tried not to get myself too worked up about it.

Just when my wrist felt like it was about to pop off, Logan jerked us to a halt. "I brought her!" he announced cheerfully.

Three distinct groups glowered down at us. When I gave Logan a raised brow, he offered me a toothy grin, his teeth still having those wolfish sharp points to them. "These are my allies. If you were on the fence about it, I wanted you to meet the most powerful supernatural entities in Fortune Academy! Trust me. You want to be my ally."

I looked back at the groups. On the far left stood students with disturbing dark eyes as if their pupils had overgrown the irises. Even their uniforms were dark and their leader stood out from among them. I recognized his voice immediately.

"Are you Lily? Logan has been talking about you all morning."

The voice belonged to the Dark Mage Hendrik and he was nothing at all what I'd expected. He was absolutely stunning and my spine straightened under the scrutiny of his eerie gaze. Like the other Dark Mages in his group, I couldn't see any color in his eyes, just an onyx-blackness that drew me in. Thick, sleek strands of midnight hair were cut short and practical, leaving the hard lines of his jaw and collarbone on full display.

"Good things, I hope," I finally answered, swallowing.

The Dark Mage swept his gaze over me again and I wondered if he could recognize me from whatever vision he'd had. If I became his ally, maybe I could hear more about it, assuming he hadn't already figured out who I was. I wanted to know what it was he'd seen. Whatever was in that vision had been powerful enough to drive Dante to track me down and make me a member of Fortune Academy. Curiosity swelled in my chest and I decided that maybe allying myself with Logan and his friends would benefit me.

There were two other groups for me to consider, however. Hendrik's group of Dark Mages were intimidating enough, but beside them stood what I guessed was Logan's wolf pack. They adopted Logan's penchant for barely being dressed and looked like they'd tossed on whatever uniform scraps they could find before walking into orientation.

Logan caught me staring at the group of muscled males and females that eyed me with reservation. "My pack stashes clothes all over campus. We're allowed to run naked except when in class."

I gave him a raised brow. "That's, uh, interesting," I said, not sure how to respond to that. The campus apparently had a clothing-optional policy until the professors had to deal with the wolves.

Glancing past the pack and to the final group, I wasn't sure what kind of supernaturals these were. Where everyone in Fortune Academy was gorgeous, these four individuals took the cake. A female crossed her arms, staring me down. Her hair ran over her shoulders in braids and her stance put a strain on her tight-fitting uniform that left little to the imagination. "Hey. I'm Ally, Daughter of Athena," she said.

I glanced back at Logan for confirmation. Leaning in, I lowered my voice. "As in... the Athena?"

Logan opened his mouth to reply, but another one of the stunning group members stepped in front of Ally. "I'm Trevor, Son of Poseidon," said a male with a stunning smile and ocean-glass eyes. He wiggled his fingers at me and droplets of water danced in the air, proving that the Greek Gods they were naming were their parents.

"I'm Zero, Son of Zeus," said a stunning and lean male who looked bored with this entire event.

Finally, the most eye-catching of the group introduced himself. "Orion," he said with a smirk. "Not sure who my father was. Probably Zeus, maybe Artemis." He shrugged. "Makes my title a little less catchy. Both my parents were such players that I never know how to introduce myself." When I blinked at him, he added, "the Demis get to keep some of our memories, so we know some of who we are and where we came from," he explained.

I couldn't help but feel a bit jealous. So, I wasn't a demi-goddess or else I would have some memory of my past. That was a bummer.

I had to take a moment to really appreciate Orion. Like his namesake, he seemed to glow from within and his eyes gleamed with golden specks matching freckles that dotted over his nose, down his arms, and I could even spot a few shining through his thin pants uniform, which I suppose was where he got his name. He looked like a constellation come to life.

Logan laughed and clapped Orion on the back. "Way to break the ice, man, but don't forget, your player ways are off-limits. I'm courting Lily here."

I choked. He really got to the point, didn't he?

"She doesn't want a wolf, bro," Orion said, flashing me a panty-melting grin. "I think she should get to choose her alliances and who she jumps around in the sheets with. What do you say, sweetheart?"

"Oh look," Melinda drawled, coming up to us and ruining my mood, "the hoe of our house has found more men to play with." Two of her posse girls sidled up behind her and gave me dagger glares.

"What do you want, Melinda?" Logan asked, sounding bored. "I'm courting Lily here, so if you have something to say about her, you'll say it in front of the group."

Melinda grinned as if she had dirt on me that would destroy my reputation before I even had a chance to build one. "She's already shacking up with a bounty hunter. Saw him go into her room just last night." She tossed a lock of glossy hair over her shoulder as she settled a smug look on her face. "Didn't think wolves liked to share outside of your pack, but that's your call, I suppose."

Logan frowned, but didn't say anything. He'd been in my bedroom all night and he knew that I hadn't slept with Dante, but to my relief, he didn't say anything.

"It's time to begin!" Gwen said with excitement bubbling in her voice that magically carried to every student in the orientation hall.

Groups began forming neat lines to the stage to go up to the fountain that Gwen had materialized. I watched to see the first group go and was relieved that there were no daggers involved. My dark secret would be kept for a little while longer yet.

What did unnerve me though was how each student reacted as they leaned over the edge of the fountain and peered into the waters. Gwen and Merlin monitored each one, documenting whatever they saw and then announcing it to the rest of the group.

"Shifter!" Merlin bellowed when one sheepish girl leaned away from the fountain, her face ashen with whatever she'd seen. In that instant her eyes flashed and sliced into the shape of a cat's. She winced and patted at her face, but her friends nudged her aside.

Logan drew in a hiss. "Oh man, a cat. I feel sorry for the newbies stuck with that crowd."

I rolled my eyes. "Weren't you one of the bullies chasing a poor cat around campus today?"

He chuckled. "Hey, it's just the natural order of things, babe. Dogs chase cats, right?"

I shrugged. "I've seen cats chase dogs before. You'd better watch who you pick on."

He gave me a toothy grin full of fang and danger and eased closer to me. His sweet musk swept over me and I tried not to respond to it as my nostrils flared. "I'll be sure to be careful," he promised. "I would never judge a supernatural by her appearance." His gaze raked over me. "No matter how delicious her appearance might be."

The various groups took their turns at the basin. Melinda already knew what she was and had solidified her alliances with a bunch of wanna-be girls, but she took her turn with giddy delight as if she had no idea what the fountain would show her. She leaned over the edge and peered in, gasping and giggling when it was over and Merlin announced her as a Muse.

I couldn't help but notice the hush that swept over the crowd. "Is a muse a bad thing?" I whispered to Logan.

He leaned in, his hot breath tickling my ear. "Supernaturals don't get much more powerful than the muses, other than the Demis." His hand found the small of my back and drew agonizing circles. "I wonder what you are that you can resist a muse's compulsion. I bet you're a Demi, too."

Even though I knew that was impossible, a shiver of

excitement swept through me as Logan guided me up the steps.

It was my turn. Okay, moment of truth.

Merlin and Gwen peered down at me over the arch of their noses as if they weren't sure what to make of me.

"You must be a new addition," Gwen said with a fragile smile as she held up her clipboard. "I didn't have you on the list. What was your name?"

I cleared my throat. "Lily Fallen." Of course, I didn't really know what my last name was. Jess had given it to me as a joke and it had just kind of stuck. It was because the first time we'd met I'd fallen flat on my face. Not the most graceful way to earn my name, but I didn't mind it so much now. I didn't have much left of Jess and it was a good memory to hold onto.

Gwen frowned at her list and I started to fidget. She flipped a few pages and then her face relaxed. "Ah, here we are. Kaito added you as a last-minute addition. I'll have to talk to him later about proper procedure, but let's proceed, shall we?"

Merlin nodded and gestured to the fountain. "It won't hurt. Simply look into the waters and tell us what you see."

I looked down at the crowd, half-hoping to see if Dante was there to offer encouragement. He wasn't there, but Logan waved at me with a giant smile on his face. I wasn't his girl, but the pride beaming from him could have suggested otherwise.

The group of Dark Mages behind him scowled, as if they expected me to somehow fail, although I didn't know how one failed an assessment.

The Demis looked bored and I assumed they were here on the off-chance another Demi was named to join their small ranks. Orion blew me a kiss, making me blush and turn back to the fountain.

"Here it goes," I whispered as my heart fluttered in my chest. This was my moment of truth. This was when I was finally going to get some answers, whether I liked it or not.

I leaned over the water and... nothing. My reflection stared back at me. I leaned further and furrowed my brows. After a ridiculous amount of waiting, I finally leaned back and offered Merlin an apologetic shrug. "I don't think it's working."

Gwen put down her clipboard and for the first time her smile disappeared.

Merlin turned to the crowd and announced the verdict. "It seems we have the day's first dud."

DUD DUTY

I WAS A DUD.

"What the fuck does that mean?" I shrieked.

Merlin turned and raised an eyebrow at me. Okay, so maybe I wasn't demonstrating the best behavior on my first day to the most influential people in Fortune Academy, but the man just called me a dud. And not just that, but he'd announced it in front of a room of hundreds of judgmental supernaturals who were all eyeing me with varying degrees of pity mixed with disgust.

"It just means that we have to bring your powers out, dear," Gwen said with a reassuring smile. "We don't get duds often, but we've gotten enough that we know what to do to help you. Your supernatural gifts need a little bit of assistance in coming out." She rested a gentle touch on my arm. "Don't worry."

Merlin scribbled something on a notepad and

handed me the slip. "Here's your counselor. Talk to her and she'll get you set up with the necessary arrangements."

Taking the piece of paper, I turned it around and frowned at it. He might as well have given me a doctor's note with some gibberish on it.

I opened my mouth to ask who my counselor was, and probably insult Merlin and his penmanship in the process, but Logan trotted up to the stage and yanked me down. "Come on," he whispered. "Don't let them see you sweat."

When we mingled back into the group I had the feeling that being a dud was just as exciting as it sounded by the pitying looks on their faces.

"I won't be allied to a dud," Hendrik growled. "You're on your own, Logan, and if you choose to keep her around, consider the wolves' alliance with the Dark Mages nullified."

Whimpers came from the wolves, but Logan showed his teeth. "Make your threats, Hendrik, but you know very well that being a dud could mean she's even more powerful than you."

"Or," Melinda drawled, looking far too pleased about this outcome, "it could mean that her supernatural side is so far regressed up her ass that she might as well be mortal."

Logan snarled and took a step in front of me. "She

resists your muse voodoo, doesn't she? You know very well that she's not mortal."

I shoved Logan aside. "I don't need you to defend me," I insisted as I took my stance against the group of supernaturals who looked positively offended by my presence. "Look, I didn't want to make alliances anyway," I said and held up my slip of paper. "Just tell me what the hell this says and I'll be on my way, all right?"

Orion leaned in and squinted at the slip, then chuckled. "Aphrodite's tits, you've been assigned to Miss Williams." He swept his fingers through his glimmering hair that seemed to sway with an invisible breeze meant only for him. "She's a real hard-ass. Good luck banishing your dud status being assigned to her."

Frowning, I crossed my arms. "Just tell me where she is."

Logan's fingers found their place at the small of my back again. "I'll take you. All the counselors are on the outskirts in the short buildings."

That's where I'd met with Kaito.

I shrugged off his touch. I wasn't going to make myself a target by forcing Logan to break alliances with some of the most powerful supernaturals in the Academy just because he'd gotten attached to me.

"I know where that is," I murmured and stuffed the slip of paper into my skirt pocket. "I'll go by myself.

I'm sure you have classes of your own to get to anyway."

Logan looked like a puppy I'd just kicked and I kind of hated myself for rejecting him, but Hendrik seemed to approve. He rested a hand on the wolf's shoulder. I flinched as the air snapped and faint purple motes drifted from Logan's skin and filtered into the Dark Mage's pendant he wore around his neck. No one else seemed to notice it, but this Dark Mage was feeding off of Logan's suffering.

"The dud is trying to do you a favor," Hendrik told Logan, digging his fingers into the wolf's shoulder. "Don't wolves mate for life? Don't shackle yourself to a sinking stone." He flashed me a grin that said he was enjoying this far too much. "Now be a good little dud and scurry on out of here."

That was my chance to escape, but some irrational part of my brain wasn't going to let Hendrik talk to me that way or take advantage of Logan's pain. I stormed up to him and ripped his hand off of Logan's shoulder. "Only if you'll be a good little douche and stop feeding on my friend." At the look of surprise that crossed his face I knew I'd hit the mark. "Isn't feeding on life-force a life-sucking trait? Would you perhaps feel more at home at Monster Academy?"

"Daaaaamn," Ally drawled, biting into her fist to suppress a laugh. "Dud's able to see your magic,

Hendrik. Even us Demis can't see that." She gave me a nod of approval. "I say let's see if Miss Williams can bring out her nature. Maybe she's actually one of us."

Hendrik growled and clutched onto his necklace. "I don't have time for this shit," he muttered and then his lips moved, but no sound came out.

A tingling filled my chest and I could have sworn his pendant glowed, but then it went dark as if I'd imagined it.

Shaking my head, I decided that I had definitely had enough of alpha supernaturals right about now and some fresh air would do me some good. "Well, off I go," I announced and turned my back on all of them.

Melinda's cackles disappeared behind me as I made my way through the crowd. I'd never felt so alone in all my life.

It took me two tries of meandering around the endless streets of Fortune Academy until I dumbly realized that the paths branched out from the epicenter which was the Central Hall. Circular streets repeated alternate patterns that were logical once I got the hang of it.

When I finally stumbled upon the familiar path to

the Freshman Dormitories, I walked past shifter tree forts until I reached the Dark Mage onyx spires. I kept going, finding that there was one last path that ran in a long arc that took me to a series of small golden buildings.

Bingo.

Approaching the entrance, I placed my hand up to the pad and let myself in. A few other students eyed me nervously and I figured I must be in the right place.

My people... the duds. Dante would be so proud.

I looked at the sign on the wall with names and office numbers. Miss Williams was on the second floor so I found the stairs and made my way up. Half of the lost looking souls in the lobby followed me.

"Dud duty?" a sheepish girl asked.

I gave her a nod. "Yep."

She let out a sigh of relief and clutched onto the rail as she climbed the steps beside me. "I thought I was the only one at first, but looks like there are quite a few of us." She glanced back at the crowd of students who seemed engrossed in watching their feet as they followed us. "We've been gathering for a few days now. There have been orientation classes all week and I come here, but no one can read the slips."

I snickered. "Of course." This place was a shit show. "But hey," I said and shrugged. "We'll get it sorted out.

Nothing to be ashamed of. It's not like we can control being duds, right?"

She brightened. "Right." She bobbed her head. "So, uh, I'm Olivia."

"Lily," I responded and gave her a quick smile.

Dante had said that I needed to build alliances. Here was a whole untapped group of potential. Maybe Logan and his hot alliance trio was an obvious choice, but I had a feeling that group came with their own agenda. I needed people I could count on.

So if established groups of supernaturals who thought they were the best thing since sliced bread were bad news, maybe I should go for the opposite. Being a dud didn't mean I was mortal and neither did it mean anyone else here was weak. I knew I was strong, but my powers were probably affected by whatever Kaito had done to me. What if someone like Olivia also had binds on her? Maybe it was a stretch, but I'd rather look for allies I could count on.

I felt more confident marching around with my army of duds, as ridiculous a notion as that was. Having the small comfort of others counting on me made me feel like I wasn't so worthless.

I found Miss Williams's door and knocked. She opened it and her eyes widened at the crowd behind me. "Are you all duds?" she asked bluntly, holding up a coffee mug and a pastry looking like she was ready to dig in to a late breakfast rather than deal with a bunch of students.

I pulled out my slip of paper and handed it to her, hoping she would know what to do with Merlin's gibberish.

Olivia did the same, followed by the group behind us as they produced their own scribbled verdicts.

Miss Williams sighed and put down her mug, then collected the slips one at a time and paired us off by numbers between one and three.

"You're a one," she told me, "a dud through and through. Your Awakening will take some patience, but we'll get you there." Miss Williams gave me a flat smile that I think was supposed to be encouraging.

I was glad to see that Olivia was a one as well. The rest were twos or threes and had shown enough glimmer in their orientation verdicts to be placed in less "ambitious" Awakening classes, whatever that meant.

It felt good to walk with Olivia through the crowds. She felt safe, whereas Dante had made me want to jump his bones just by the proximity of his heat and Logan just had me confused.

"Are you nervous?" Olivia asked as we followed the color-coded map Miss Williams had given us. Finally, I didn't feel like I was going to get hopelessly lost on campus. I'd missed the miniature lights in the street entirely that marked which branch of the circle we were on and where we needed to go.

I turned and followed the trail of lights that would take us on the opposite side of Central Hall. We had to take the long way around the spire, but I didn't mind. It gave me some time to think. "Not nervous," I admitted. "Just ready to figure out what I am."

She chuckled and clutched her map to her chest, subtly showing me that she trusted me to guide us in the right direction. "You and me both. I've been here nearly a week and no one will talk to me ever since I was announced as a dud." She presented her arms. "I mean, did they tattoo it on us? It's like everyone knows."

I smirked. Little did she know how close to the truth she was in my case. But in her situation, I knew what gave her away. She slunk around and kept her head low. Every other supernatural in this place was cocky and knew where they belonged. Her body language said it all. "Any idea what you might be?" I asked, trying to strike up a conversation.

She shrugged and fell into step closer to me, as if just talking about her potential supernatural powers put her on edge. "Not really, but I do have these really weird dreams that I'm drowning. It's pretty messed up."

Poor girl was probably stressed. I squeezed her shoulder. "Well don't worry. I'm sure those are just dreams.

Once you find out what you are then you can show all those douchebags what they've been missing out on."

She grinned. "You mean we can, right? We're totally going to be our own alliance."

I laughed. "Dud alliance. I like it."

The trail of lights eventually led us down Demigod street. Luckily our classes were closest to the Central Hall and I wouldn't have to see where Orion was holed up and have that thrown in my face. I pictured a miniature Olympus with floating cherubs or some shit. There was no way I was a Demi and I wasn't interested in being one either.

We met up with some other level one duds in the lobby and were eventually greeted by a panther shifter who'd come to fetch us. Unlike the wolves, she wore an immaculate fitting of her uniform and clearly didn't shift unless she absolutely had to. The only damning evidence of what she was showed by her sliced pupils that cut through emerald irises. "Level one duds with me," she said, her words having a low rumble to them as if she wanted to be anywhere else but here.

Olivia and I shared a look and then followed the panther shifter until we arrived at a classroom.

I wasn't sure what I expected. Maybe some desks and a whiteboard like any other typical classroom, but that's not what waited for us inside.

This looked more like a gladiator ring. Weapons of

all sorts lined the walls and the center had a sandpit with a wide ring around it. The boundary had spiked pins sticking up from the floor, promising anyone thrown out of the ring would pay for that failure.

"The hell is this?" I muttered to Olivia.

The girl hugged herself and looked at her feet. "I've heard about the Awakening process. It's... partly why I pretended I couldn't find Miss William's office for so long."

"Welcome to your Awakening," the panther shifter said dryly and she rubbed her ear with the back of her hand, then seemed to catch herself in the non-human motion and put her hand firmly at her side. "Professor Payne will be here to walk you through—ah there he is."

A miniature man I might have mistaken for a dwarf sauntered into the room. I knew there were undocumented supernaturals, but I wasn't so sure about fairy-tales come to life.

Professor Payne sure fit the part, though. He glowered at all of us through beady eyes alight with determination that we were going to leave here "awakened," or die trying. "Okay, duds," he said, his voice booming through the room as he stalked towards what looked like a glorified highchair. He settled himself onto it and gripped both armrests as he frowned, the gesture making his beard puff out like a spiked animal on full alert. "You have supernatural heritage or else you wouldn't have been accepted into Fortune Academy." He leaned in, glaring at us. Some of the duds cowered closer to the wall, but Olivia and I stood our ground. The small defiance awarded us with the professor's full attention. "What is not so fortunate is that your minds are suppressing your supernatural gifts." He leaned back, seeming satisfied with the chastisement. "This just means we need to retrain your minds to accept who and what you are. All will be revealed in time. It will take pain. It will take effort, and it will take a heavy dose of fear."

"Fear?" Olivia squeaked.

Professor Payne nodded. "That's right. Survival instincts are what will trigger your defense mechanisms, so we need to bring those out. We could poke and pry using magic, but the simplest and most effective way is to force you to defend yourself." He pointed at the arena. "You two. Fight to the death."

Olivia and I froze and a gasp swept out behind us as the other duds pressed even harder against the wall.

Death? What kind of academy was this?

"Forgive me for asking," I began, taking a step closer to the professor in his mighty highchair, "but if we fight to the death then doesn't that sort of defeat the purpose? Not much "Awakening" to be done if we're dead."

He chuckled, sending his beard puffing in new directions like a happy dog that hadn't had a haircut all his life. "This is a magic room. You can't actually die here, but it'll feel like it." He waved a hand at the weapons and they began to glow. "Each of these are imbued with powerful spells. The Dark Mages fuel the Awakening trials with their gifts. It's part of the contribution of blood duty given as demerits to other students."

I hadn't had a chance to read my welcome packet yet, but I made a mental note to scour it for information. Blood duty... Dante had mentioned that before to Hendrik. By chopping off his hand, Hendrik would have enough power to be exempt from blood duty for a week, whatever that meant.

The cat shifter clapped her hands. "Enough wasting time. We need to kill at least half of you before lunch, so chop-chop." She smirked at her terrible pun.

Rolling my eyes, I walked into the center of the arena. Olivia trailed after me with her feet dragging lines in the sand.

"Weapon of choice?" Professor Payne asked me.

If I chose my weapon first, it might give Olivia a chance to choose something that would properly defend against it. I didn't want to kill her, even if it was fake. I was sure no matter how powerful the spell, death would feel real enough.

As I looked over the crossbows, spears, and swords, a wave of dread swept over me. This just felt... wrong.

"And if we refuse?" I countered, propping my hands on my hips to glare at the dwarf.

He leaned back and regarded me with a smug look while he settled into his highchair, which might as well have been a throne that said we were in his domain now. "You're free to leave the Academy, if that's what you wish, however we can't have untapped and undocumented supernaturals running around humanity. There are certain... binds that'll make you more or less human, if that's what you really want."

"No," Olivia said, her voice firm. "I want to do this." I turned to regard her and a pang of sympathy hit my chest. I recognized the look on her face. She was just as lost as I was. She was here to discover who and what she was after losing her memory of any history, family, or sense of homecoming. The panic in her eyes said that if she didn't get that chance, she'd never be able to live with herself.

I could relate.

"Dagger," I said instinctively. I hadn't yet decided if I was going to let Olivia win, but there were plenty of weapon choices that could give her an advantage.

She looked through her options, her gaze scanning over the spear that would give her better reach, but perhaps be clumsy. The sword would also allow her to keep her distance, but might be too heavy. Finally, her attention rested on the crossbow.

"That one," she said, pointing to the ranged weapon. It was a risky choice, but I approved. I was good with a dagger and if Olivia could take me out before I had a chance to get in up close, she might win on her own accord.

The panther shifter collected the weapons and tossed them into the arena. They glowed with power and the sands reacted, resonating with the spell that would hopefully keep us alive when one emerged the victor.

I took up my dagger and tested its weight, then raised both my eyebrows at Olivia as if to say, you sure about this?

She slung the bolt quiver over her shoulder and nocked one bolt into her crossbow, then gave me a jerky nod. "I'm ready."

Professor Payne raised up one hand. "Everyone pay attention. If we're lucky, one of these ladies will Awaken." He regarded us with a stern stare. "If either of you hesitates or gives up, the magic will take hold and force a winner. Don't let it come to that." He balled his fingers into a fist and jerked down. "Begin!"

Magic popped me in the legs and startled me into a slow, stalking circle around the perimeter of the arena.

Olivia's knees buckled, but then she straightened them and aimed the crossbow at me.

Olivia had seemed sheepish and weak this whole time, but the promise that she might find out what she was seemed to drive her into a deeper personality hidden underneath the mortal exterior. Deep down, she was supernatural, just like me and everyone else here.

I couldn't help but smile. As barbaric as the arena might be, it looked like the process of Awakening was already working on her.

I, on the other hand, didn't feel anything different other than the razor edge of fear that ran up my spine at having a weapon pointed at me. I angled my feet and bent my knees. When Olivia let her first bolt loose, I twisted out of the way and the breeze of the deadly weapon whizzed inches away from my face.

Too close for comfort.

Professor Payne was right about one thing. Survival instinct kicked in and I launched closer to Olivia, hoping to catch her off-guard before she nocked another bolt that she was already trying to saddle into the weapon. Her eyes glowed with determination and very real magic. Whatever she was underneath the surface was trying to come out.

"That's it," Professor Payne said with approval. "Keep going. It's working."

I thrust with my dagger, but Olivia twisted and shot a fresh bolt. Pain laced through my shoulder and I cried out as I went launching back. As if being impaled by a bolt wasn't bad enough, I fell at the edge of the arena's border and my hand landed on the spiked boundary, impaling me to the bone.

Pain made my vision haze red.

Then panic set in.

Would the others see my blood? Did it run black?

I glanced at my mangled hand, growing queasy at the sight of spikes running through flesh, but I didn't bleed. The magic of the Arena hummed through my wounds. Kaito and Dante wouldn't have let me come here if my cover would have been blown. Bile rose in my throat that they might have known I'd come here... and accepted I might die for the sake of "Awakening."

How kind of them...

Olivia grimaced at my whimper as I unlatched my hand from the spikes and she lowered her crossbow, but the magic of the arena wasn't going to allow mercy. Her arms shot up as she aimed again, this time her eyes filled with panic. "Lily," she cried out, "move!"

Damn it.

I rolled out of the way as she let another bolt fly. It sank into the sands and I used the only supernatural ability to have manifested in myself so far to propel myself halfway across the arena. My supernatural strength could be from any of the magical manifestations I'd seen in the Academy and didn't give me a clue as to what I was, but right now, I didn't care. My emotions and logic filtered out a small window in my mind and only instinct remained.

Kill or be killed.

Survive.

My dagger found its mark and Olivia shrieked, grabbing at the hilt of the blade now buried in her abdomen. Her eyes flashed with purple magic and the hairs over my entire body stood on end as she reached out and gripped my arm. "Lily," she said, repeating my name.

Foam pooled at her mouth and sanity came flooding back to me. "Oh gods, Olivia. I'm so sorry," I whimpered as guilt and dread made my hands shake.

She didn't react how I expected. She smiled and her glowing eyes drooped with satisfaction. "I know... what I am."

Olivia fell over onto the sands with a final thud.

Silence.

I stared at her, waiting for the magic to bring her back to life, but she didn't move. I shot up a panicked glance at the dwarf. "Professor Payne?" I pressed.

He narrowed his eyes and waited, then after what felt like an eternity, he lifted one hand. The panther shifter took an orb from her pocket and broke it in her fist, sending a *whoosh* to sweep through the room.

Olivia drew in a desperate gasp and I let go of the breath I'd been holding. "Oh gods, Olivia," I cried, crawling to her and rolling her onto my thighs. I ran my fingers through her sweat-dampened hair. "I'm so sorry. Are you okay? Does it... hurt?"

Her eyes still aglow, she glanced up at me and smiled.

"Am I okay?" She lifted herself up and giggled, showing me the runes that flashed all over her body in vibrant swirls. "Lily! I'm a fucking Dark Mage!"

My hands fell to the sands and I tried to be happy for her. "Wow, Olivia. That's really great."

I didn't feel any differently, and even though Olivia was the one who'd died, I felt like the one who'd been stabbed straight in the heart.

When would I ever find out what the hell I was?

A TRUE FRIEND

I DIDN'T HAVE MUCH OF AN APPETITE AFTER murdering my first and only real friend at Fortune Academy, but Olivia was in the mood to celebrate. We'd been handed our welcome packets we would have gotten at orientation had we not been duds, as well as new schedules. Mine was an indefinite repeat of the Awakening Arena, once per day, with mandatory meetings with a counselor of my choice. They probably expected me to talk with Miss Williams, but it would give me a good excuse to go see Kaito later.

Still, I wished that I'd been Awakened too as something normal like a Dark Mage. I had a feeling when my powers finally came to light they wouldn't have neat classes lined up to walk me through my development.

"Don't look so depressed!" Olivia chimed, looping her arm with mine and dragging me down the street towards the cafeteria that better resembled a gothic castle than a place where the campus came to eat lunch. "I finally know what I am!"

"But how did it happen?" I asked, still dazed by the whole experience. "I mean, didn't it hurt?"

She shrugged, her bony shoulder bumping into mine. "Well, yeah, it hurt a lot." She stuck a finger in my uniform hole where her bolt had pierced me. "Bet that hurt, too."

It wasn't even comparable. The magic of the arena had healed both of us, but she'd still fucking died. I never felt more like a monster than I did right then.

"Hey," Olivia said, her voice softening as she tugged me to a halt, "don't look so guilty, okay?" Her eyes still held that mystical purple glow as if she'd been suppressing her magic all her life and there was so much it was just shining out of her with the force of a minia-ture sun. She smiled, that joy in her beaming unlike anything I'd seen before. "I am more than thrilled. You have no idea what I've been going through..." She chuck-led. "Well, I guess you do. I'm sorry. Here I am wanting to celebrate and you still don't know what you are."

I waved away her concern. "That's not a big deal. I'm sure I'll figure it out soon enough." Of course the big question was eating at me, but a part of me was relieved, too. Whatever I was couldn't be good. I doubted I was anything this school had ever seen or else Dante wouldn't have gone through so much trouble to track me down. Hendrik wouldn't have had a vision of me that had set all of this in motion. No, maybe it was a good thing I didn't know what I was yet. I'd find out soon enough and then my life would change forever.

"Are you hungry?" she asked. As much as she wanted to celebrate, I thought it was sweet that Olivia was more concerned about my emotional well-being. "We could go back to the dorms if you prefer. I have some snacks."

"No, that's okay." I tugged her towards the cafeteria again and my stomach released a growl that had us both giggling. "The dorms are too far away for my stomach to handle, I'm pretty sure."

We ventured inside with our arms interlocked and it felt good, almost like this was a real university and I was finding a place where I could belong. Olivia didn't know how much she grounded me and we'd only just met. It felt good to have a friend.

The roar of the cafeteria hit us hard when we stepped inside. The voices echoed off of the unforgiving onyx, reminding me of the Dark Mage dormitories, and I glanced up at the rows of looming statues. "This place is creepy," I said loud enough for Olivia to hear me over the din.

She chuckled and took a big whiff. "But it smells delicious!"

She was right. Stations of every kind of food imaginable lined the walls and mouth-watering scents drifted over the crowd, making my stomach pinch with hunger. It felt like I hadn't eaten in forever.

We bypassed a station clearly intended for shifters with raw meat served both bloody or cooked on a spit. A funnel drew most of the smoke through an escape vent, but enough of the aroma from the cooking meat made me want to pause. One of the shifters from Logan's pack glared at me, so I tugged Olivia to keep walking.

Similar glares followed at each station. Golden fruit at the Demi counter came paired with a snub from Trevor who was eating fish whole. Then the dark magic counter which had black apples looked as if they might let us join now that Olivia's powers had emerged, but the second we got close a group of Dark Mages barreled into us and sent me reeling to the floor.

Olivia helped me up. "Do I have something on my face?" I asked. "What gives? Why won't they let us get food?"

I was starting to get pissed off.

Olivia cast a nervous glance around the room and her nostrils flared. "It's hard to tell over the food... but I think... I smell a spell." She looked at a station tucked at the end of the line. "Let's just eat at the dud counter. I've been eating there all week and it's fine."

I wanted to protest, but now that I paused to focus,

Olivia was right. That hum in my chest had grown and it seemed to resonate with everyone around us.

This was Hendrik's doing.

I wasn't going to get this resolved by fighting off a bunch of spelled people. I'd face the Dark Mage bastard later. For now, I needed to get my energy reserves up, which meant food. "Yeah, okay," I relented.

The dud counter wasn't half-bad. It was the same kind of comfort food Jess and I would indulge in sometimes when we were in a hurry. I picked out an oversized slice of pepperoni pizza and Olivia got a grilled cheese sandwich.

Finding a place to sit was almost as much fun as finding a counter that would serve us. The cafeteria was so crowded and the long mahogany tables boasted cliques that had no intention of sharing a spot with us. My gaze raked over piles of shifters, Dark Mages, and a bunch of girls with perfected resting bitch faces which I assumed were Melinda's crew.

We finally opted for a small lopsided table in the corner next to a trash bin. I slammed my tray down and glared at the rest of the room as if I could set the entire cafeteria on fire. "This is total bullshit," I complained, then sat down and folded my pizza in half and shoved it into my face.

What can I say. I was hungry.

Olivia chuckled and elegantly took her seat. She took

one half of the sliced sandwich and pinched it between her fingers before nibbling on the end. "So, who did you piss off?" she asked, her deepening dark eyes gleaming with excitement. "It's got to be a Dark Mage. Make some enemies at the dorms already? I bet I can take her on."

I took another gigantic bite of my pizza, leaving half of it remaining. I set it down and wiped my mouth with a napkin. "*Him*, not her," I corrected around my mouthful. "Hendrik."

Olivia had been taking a sip of her water when I'd said that and she choked on it. "Hendrik?" she gasped, setting the bottle down and gripping the weak plastic until it threatened to crumple and its insides overflow all over the table.

I scratched at the invisible runes on my arms. If only Kaito hadn't bound my powers maybe none of this would be happening, but if he hadn't... no telling what orientation or the Awakening Arena might have revealed. "I might have pissed Hendrik off at orientation," I said with a shrug. "One of the wolf shifters is courting me and Hendrik didn't like the idea of his ally being stuck with me. Apparently wolves mate for life, or some shit."

Olivia leaned in, clearly captivated by the whole thing. "Which wolf shifter? The only one I'd imagine that Hendrik would care about would be the pack leader, but no way he'd be courting anyone, much less one of us duds." She grimaced. "Well, no offense. You know what I mean."

I scratched harder at my arm even though it was starting to burn. "Leader?" I couldn't see Logan leading anyone out of a paper bag. "What's the wolf pack leader's name?" I ventured.

She pointed over my shoulder. "He's actually right there."

I turned to find Logan staring straight at me. He was his usual primal, gorgeous self. At least he wasn't naked, but he still wore his blazer and tie over his bare chest followed by his loose-fitting pants that had my eyes roaming along the guiding lines of muscle. He pattered towards us, not wearing any shoes. "You have some nerve showing your face," he growled.

I gave the last of my pizza a wistful look before getting out of my chair to face the wolf. "Excuse me?" I countered. "Since when do you talk to me like that? I thought you were courting me."

Olivia gave a gasp, but I ignored her.

Logan was in a mood, apparently, because he shoved me against the wall and slammed both fists on either side of my face. Even though the cafeteria was packed, an immediate hush descended on our small corner.

Something in Logan's eyes wasn't right. Rage burned in him that didn't make sense and every muscle in his body quivered as if he was resisting a shift. His mouth parted, taking in my scent as his nostrils flared. His eyes flashed up to meet mine. "You've been fucking the hunter," he snarled. "I was courting you until I found out you were just like the rest. A fucking *slut*."

I shoved him—hard. Every ounce of my supernatural strength sent him flailing away from me and I was glad I had something to work with. This dud wasn't a total loser.

"You know I'm not sleeping with Dante," I said, keeping my voice calm as I lowered it so only he could hear me. "Remember? You were in my room all night. Nobody else was there."

He blinked a few times as if he was confused, then shook his head. "No," he snapped. "Hendrik told me the truth."

A noise of frustration escaped me. "Logan, seriously. I'm not sleeping with him, and even if I was, it's not really any of your business anyway. I didn't *ask* you to court me!"

He straightened. "Don't worry about that anymore. We're done. I'll leave you to my allies." He glanced at Olivia and lifted his lip with a sneer. "Looks like you have a pet Dark Mage. Doubt she'll be able to protect you from the wrath of Fortune Academy's finest."

My mouth parted with silent shock as he turned and left, revealing who'd been watching from the sidelines behind him. Hendrik, Orion, and a bunch of snarling wolf-shifters circled around us, making me feel hopelessly pinned between a wall and a mass of angry supernaturals.

Olivia edged closer to me. She hadn't let go of her grilled cheese this whole time and she took another nibble as she assessed the situation. "Well, my guess is Hendrik's spell has come to full effect and it was between you and Logan, but it's affected everyone he's come into contact with." She narrowed her eyes. "It's fascinating. I can see the tiny threads connecting everyone. It's a powerful spell. Where did he get that kind of energy?"

I wanted to scream. From chopping off Dante's hand, of course.

Orion approached me first, paired with a girl on each arm as if for effect to remind me how desirable he was, as if his godly good looks weren't enough to rub that fact in my face. "Now that we know you're a dud, you're only good for one thing." He waggled his eyebrows at me. "I'm having an orgy party tomorrow night. You're welcome to... *come*." He licked his lips on the last word.

I balled my fingers into a fist and took a swing at him, aiming straight for his perfect nose. The blow landed—hard.

"Are you insane?" I ground through clenched teeth as he stumbled back and the girls on his arm fluttered away with gasps of horror. "If Hendrik's spell is working on you, then you're even dumber than you look."

I meant it as an insult, but he took that as a compliment. Orion looked up at me with a grin as a trickle of bright red blood rolled over his lips. So, gods bled too. "Oh, spells don't work on me, darling." He gave me a wink. "But I'm glad you think I'm dumb. That'll make outsmarting you into my bed so much more satisfying."

He sauntered off and Olivia released a low whistle, which was severely impeded by the dried crumbs from her sandwich. "Damn. I've never seen anyone get under a Demi's skin, much less punch one in the face, but Orion seemed pretty shaken."

I gave her a raised brow. "Uh, really? He looked fine to me."

Hendrik interrupted us by tossing an orb to the ground. Purple smoke made me gag and Olivia dropped her sandwich in disgust. A magical stink bomb, really, so mature. "You two get this straight," he said, snapping a finger at us. "You've gotten on my bad side, which means you're going to have to get in line and grovel for my forgiveness. You don't eat unless I say you can eat. You don't fuck unless I say you can fuck. And you don't even breathe unless I say you can." He snapped his fingers and Olivia clutched at her throat.

"Olivia?" I cried and grabbed onto her arm as she sank to her knees. "Hendrik, stop it!"

He smirked, although there was a gleam of hatred in his eyes. I had a feeling that his choking spell was supposed to have affected me too. A simple stink bomb might work on me, but something that actually threatened my willpower or my life bounced right off of whatever defense mechanisms my body had in place, the same ones that worked against Melinda's attempts to compel me.

"It's sweet you've made a baby alliance," Hendrik said, lowering his voice with a dangerous growl that would have been sexy had I not known that he spent his free time chopping off people's hands. "If you like this little Dark Mage, then you'll do as I say, got it? She's one of my clan, which means she owes a blood debt to her people." His dark eyes flashed with malice and triumph. He knew he had something I wanted to protect— Olivia. "What I say goes and you're going to have to accept that." He hooked the collar of my torn uniform and made me stand on my tiptoes. "These are my orders. You're going to partake in your new friend's blood debt, then you're to stay away from Logan and any member of my alliance unless you are specifically called upon." He sniffed at Olivia. "That includes any pathetic excuses of an alliance you manage to build as well."

I was already indebted to Olivia for the suffering I'd put her through. I'd fucking killed her, and now I'd put her on Hendrik's bad side. It made me regret ever opening up to her. If I'd just been mean or distant when she'd first introduced herself, none of this would be happening right now.

"If you hurt her I'll—"

Olivia made a strangled sound as Hendrik twisted his spell harder. "You'll what? You'll let your one ally die over your pride?"

I balled my fingers into fists, cutting my palms with the crescents of my fingernails. "Fine," I said, hating how pathetic and weak I sounded. I didn't have anything to throw back at Hendrik... other than the demon conjuring orb I had in my pocket and that would do a better job of getting me expelled than accomplishing anything useful. If I really found myself in danger, it was a last resort, but now was not the time. Unfortunately, Hendrik had me in his crosshairs and he knew it. All I had to do was pretend to roll over... for now.

"I'm sorry," he said, leaning closer to me. "I didn't quite hear you." He beckoned me closer. "Why don't you whisper it in my ear so I make sure we have an understanding."

I glanced at Olivia who still clutched at her throat and her lips were taking on a shade of blue. Dammit. He wouldn't actually make her pass out... or worse, would he? By the dangerous gleam in his black eyes that sparked with power I knew better than to test him.

I moved in until I was close enough to touch him and a tingling swept over my body. His spell wouldn't work on me, but I sensed it crawling over me and my nostrils flared against the impact of the sweet scent.

Didn't Olivia say magic had a smell?

If it did, Hendrik's was roses... along with something else that tinged the edges of my senses with a metallic taste.

Blood?

That would make sense. Hendrik was a Dark Mage. His magic was based in goodness. I felt it, but the blood magic he'd swept over it changed it fundamentally in a way that was... wrong.

"I'm waiting, Lily."

Hearing him say my name made a shiver run down my spine. I forced myself to spit out what he wanted to hear.

"I'll do what you want, Hendrik. Please, don't hurt Olivia."

It was just words, but the defeat that settled into my chest made me want to vomit.

Hendrik leaned back with a smirk on his face. He waved his hand and Olivia gasped for breath, making me relax with relief.

"Good. Now, I have more important matters to attend to. You'd do well to stay out of my sight, but be sure to show up for blood duty tonight." He grinned. "My dorms. Bring your friend."

Shit, he wanted us to do blood duty today? I hoped that didn't involve losing any limbs.

"Right, okay, whatever," I promised, although I had no intention of bringing Olivia along so he could lord her life over me again.

Satisfied, Hendrik grinned and backed away. A distant crack sounded through the room as he changed the hold of his spell and I noted that a line of concentration disappeared from his forehead. The crowd dispersed as the spell weaned. "Good. I'll see you tonight then." He looked back at my sad, deflated pizza still on my tray. "Finish your... nourishment, so that you'll have the energy to donate."

When he'd stalked off I sank into my chair. I wasn't hungry anymore and my pizza was cold, but Hendrik was right about one thing. I'd need energy to survive whatever came next.

Olivia sank into her own chair opposite from me and the pulsing gleam in her dark eyes seemed weak. "Well, that sucked," she admitted.

I hummed my agreement as I numbly chewed my cold pizza. "Look, Olivia. I'm sorry. Maybe we shouldn't hang out, at least until I figure out how to deal with Hendrik."

She gripped my wrist hard, that wicked determination back in her eyes. "I'm not abandoning you, okay? I know what it's like to be a dud and feel powerless. I just need to learn my powers and then we'll have a better chance against him, *together*, okay?"

I didn't want to count on Olivia to find Hendrik's weak spot, but my heart warmed at the sentiment. "Thanks," I whispered.

No matter what happened, at least I'd found a true ally, and perhaps a real friend.

OLIVIA OFFERED to go with me to my counselor meeting, but I could see how tired she was.

"Relax," I said with a laugh. "You've actually died today. I think you deserve a break."

She pouted. "I don't really know where to go. My packet says I can choose to room with an ally in the Freshman dorms or I can relocate to the Dark Mage dormitories." She shuddered. "I really don't want to be anywhere near Hendrik right now... so would you mind... if we were roomies?"

I jerked to a halt and stared at her. I'd just resolved in my mind that Olivia and I were going to stay far away from each other, for her own safety, but the glimmer of hope that this was my excuse to hold onto my friend tugged at me. "Are you sure?" I asked. "I mean, sticking around me might be more dangerous than trying to build alliances with the Dark Mages. You only have a bad rap because of me."

She grinned. "Are you kidding? Once we kick Hendrik's ass we're going to *own* the Dark Mages. No way in hell am I going anywhere."

While her confidence in me was warming, I felt it was a bit misguided. "If you say so," I said with a chuckle. "My room is on the third floor at the end of the hall. If we hurry I can drop you off on my way to talk to my counselor." I gave her a nudge. "I'll ask about this bullshit with Hendrik saying you owe some blood debt just because you're a Dark Mage. Surely there are rules at the Academy about stuff like that."

"That's sweet of you," she said, the sheepish girl I'd met at first coming out as she tucked her head, then she smiled. "You don't have to drop me off, actually. We can blood swap and that'll let me into your room and I can get settled in, if that's okay."

I froze. Blood? No, that definitely wasn't a good idea. "I don't know," I said, grimacing. "I mean, not sure what a blood swap is. You're fine to make yourself at home."

She grabbed my hand. "I don't mean actual blood. Chill. Just give me permission to enter your room while we're holding hands and your imprint will go into my blood."

"Oh," I said, looking down at her fingers. "Uh, you have permission to enter my room."

A faint glow lit up our hands and then it faded.

"Great!" she said. "Now it's official. We're roomies!" She surprised me by launching into a full hug.

Olivia had really come a long way. When I'd first met her earlier today she was lost and broken, but the promise of awakening her supernatural nature gave her the courage to die in the Awakening Arena. Then discovering her true identity gave her back her spirit for life. I wanted to stay up all night with her and ask her what it felt like to be given back something that was taken, because no telling how or when that would ever happen for me.

Olivia and I walked hand-in-hand towards the dormitories and I decided then and there that I was going to do everything in my power to make sure I wouldn't let Olivia down.

A PROPHECY IS TOLD

Standing outside of Kaito's office, I took a moment to review my day. So much had happened already and I still didn't know who I could trust or why I'd been brought here. Hendrik might not recognize me from his vision, but I was definitely on his radar now. When would he put the pieces together? Maybe on some level that's exactly what he was trying to do. Picking on me was his way of figuring me out... and when he did, shit would hit the fan. It was excuse enough to talk to Kaito and get him to do something.

I rapped my knuckles against the wood and waited. Nothing. I tried again. "Kaito?" I ventured, then felt weird wondering if I should call him Mr. Nakamura. I glanced at his nameplate above the door. He was supernatural, so maybe he wasn't as young as he looked.

After a moment the door opened and I swallowed

hard. I'd forgotten how gorgeous he was. A long tattoo ran up his left cheek and a streak of silver followed through his hair, making me forget the urge to call him Mr. Nakamura. I wondered if he dyed the silver strands that gave him a dangerous edge or if it grew naturally that way. I didn't even know what kind of supernatural he was. "Now isn't a good time," he said. I couldn't help but notice the dark circles under his eyes and the sluggish way he leaned against the door.

I peered around him at the haphazard clutter of papers and empty coffee mugs, as well as some rolled-up wrappers on the floor that hadn't made it into the trash. "What's going on?" I raised an eyebrow. "Have you left this office at all since I last saw you?"

He ran his fingers through his hair and sighed. "Just come inside. I can't stop working. If you're going to loiter then don't draw attention to yourself."

He took his seat at his desk and began scribbling on some paperwork.

I debated if I should just leave, but decided against it and ventured inside, closing the door behind me. "So, they have me on the roster for the Awakening Arena every day," I told him. If I'd expected a reaction, I didn't get much.

"Hmm," he offered without looking up at me.

Okay, well, if he was going to pretend I didn't exist I'd just lay it all out there.

"I killed a girl in the Arena. She didn't deserve it, but it worked for her and she turned out to be a Dark Mage. Now Hendrik is saying she owes some blood debt. That's bullshit, right? And then there's this wolf, Logan, who was trying to court me. I guess that pissed off Hendrik. You know Hendrik? The Dark Mage that had a vision about me but isn't supposed to know about me? Yeah well he's all sorts of pissed off that his spells don't work on me, so is Melinda the Muse, so anyway now Hendrik has me coming over tonight for blood duty or else he'll do something bad to Olivia—my Dark Mage friend, that is. Meanwhile Dante is nowhere to be found. What I do know is that he made a bad trade with Hendrik and lost his hand and it's not growing back. Now he's missing and I don't know why he brought me here if he was just going to leave me to the wolves... literally."

Kaito had dropped his pencil during my tirade and his jaw slacked open. "Well," he said after a moment, "you've had quite the day." He leaned on his desk and rolled small circles around his temples. "Look. There are rules here. If you've made an alliance with a fledgling Dark Mage, then that's Hendrik's territory. He has a right to initiate her into his clan. It is similar to how Dark Mages work in the real world, so we allow it." When I crossed my arms and glowered at him, he sighed. "I know it's a lot, but this is the best place for you even if things don't seem fair. If Monster Academy had gotten their hands on you..." His words drifted off.

I crossed my arms. "Then what? What would have happened that you're so afraid of?" Anger washed over me. I was tired of this shit. Tired of other people hiding secrets. Tired of them telling me what to do and thinking that their problems were more important than mine. So he had a lot of paperwork. So fucking what? This was bigger than that and he needed to give me more. "Hey," I said, slamming my hands onto his desk and sending his papers fluttering in my wake. His gaze matched mine and something deep inside of me snapped. The invisible rune Kaito had placed on my left arm burned, but I ignored it. I had his attention and I tugged on it. He responded by stumbling out of his chair and leaning over the desk to grip onto my wrist.

"Lily," he said, his eyes wide, "I can't just, tell you everything. That won't help. It could just make things worse for you by telling you things I don't yet understand."

"Why?" I pressed, pulling on that invisible thread that connected us. He leaned in and I became acutely aware of how attractive he was. His Asian features made him smooth and hard in all the right places and I indulged myself by tracing his jawline with my finger. He shivered under my touch, releasing a pleasant sensation into the air. Instinct made me want to draw that nectar in, but the rune on my arm burned hot, forcing me to allow it to sweep free in the room. "Just give me something, Kaito."

His mouth parted when my finger ran over his lips, making the aroma of power flush hot in the room.

I didn't just want to know answers anymore; I wanted to taste him. Frustration bubbled inside of me that I couldn't do what it wanted because of his stupid binding runes. The least he could give me was the physical component of my sudden need.

His gaze locked onto mine and he knew what I wanted—what I demanded, and he gripped the back of my head and crushed his mouth to mine. My lips parted for him, surprised and welcoming of the warm kiss after all this time being teased and taunted by the gorgeous supernaturals that I'd met at Fortune Academy. All my frustration and impatience seeped away into sensual delight as Kaito's hard touch ran down my neck, over my shoulder, then he grazed the invisible bind on my arm and light flashed between us, sending me reeling back.

"Fuck," Kaito said, grimacing and holding a hand over his eyes. "I should have been prepared for that. I'm sorry."

Dazed, I stumbled back and fell into a chair. I didn't understand the lust that had overwhelmed me, nor why it had melted into a dull need that made me want Kaito, but was manageable now. I pinched my thighs together.

as if that might help. "I'm, uh," a wave of heat swept over my face and I touched my warmed cheek. Was I blushing? I did *not* blush.

Kaito adjusted himself before he sat on the edge of his desk. My eyes went to his crotch and I had no doubt I was blushing now. "One of your powers, one that Monster Academy wants, is banned," he began.

I bit my lip and forced myself to look up in his face. His gorgeous face that I'd just been slurping at like a piece of candy. "Let me guess," I said with defeat. "I'm part succubus."

He smirked. "Yep."

Fuck.

I BURIED my face in my hands as humiliation set in.

I was one-third succubus.

Jess would have a field day with that if I ever saw her again.

I groaned and curled my head between my legs. "I knew it. I'm a monster."

"No," Kaito said forcefully enough that I snapped up and peeked at him through my fingers. "This is precisely why I didn't want to tell you what you were.

Your supernatural powers don't define you, Lily. Your actions do."

"I made you suck my face," I countered. "That's a dick move, you know, something a *monster* might do."

He chuckled and his cheeks reddened. "I don't make much time for romances, so maybe that was a push I needed. Don't feel sorry for me, anyway." His gaze flashed to meet mine and he offered me a sexy smile that made me push my thighs together again. "There's something else that might make you feel better. You have involvement in a prophecy I've been researching, which is why Hendrik had a vision about you. Although, I don't think even he realizes what he saw yet."

I scratched at the rune that had burned me and now twinged with retaliation that I'd used my succubus powers in spite of the bind. Kaito's arousal still lingered in the air and teased me by the fact that I couldn't feed on it. "Prophecy. Great."

"Hear me out," he said, lifting a hand. "You know the Echoes of Calamity? Well, I believe that you're the one meant to face the Third Echo of Calamity that will soon be upon us."

I froze. From what I knew about the Echoes of Calamity, they were Heaven and Hell, Life and Death sort of shit. The First Echo of Calamity had broken the barrier between separate worlds, the Second had forced them to merge... I didn't even want to know what the Third Echo of Calamity was meant to do.

"You can't face an Echo of Calamity alone. That's why you will draw Virtues to you." He twisted and rummaged through the papers, producing something that was hardly legible. "That's what I've been doing. Research. All the supernaturals Awakened here bring with them memories and stories from their home realms. Each one has something in common. Each realm has a prophecy that has predicted the Echoes of Calamity and the women who will call upon their Virtues to stop it."

I frowned. "Virtues?"

He nodded, his face beaming with excitement. "Yes. It wasn't until I got a recent shifter testimony that I figured it out. Her prophecy doesn't call them Virtues, but Mates."

Mates.

I blinked a few times to make sure I'd heard him correctly. "So, you're saying that I need... mates, plural, in order to stop the end of the world?"

He chuckled and ran his fingers through his hair, upsetting the perfect silver line that ran through his temple. "Well, yeah. That's exactly what I'm saying, so the fact that you have succubus gifts doesn't actually surprise me. It's meant to help you draw your Virtues... your mates, to you." He looked down at the paper and an adorable smile lifted the corners of his lips. "I'm honored to accept your advances because that means I'm one of them, Lily. I'm one of the intended guardians to help you grow your power, strengthen your resolve, and by standing by your side, stop the end of the world."

I didn't know much about Kaito, not yet, but I got the sense that this was the culmination of his life's work, but I didn't just want to be a means to an end, even for someone like Kaito. If I took a mate, or... *mates*, then it was going to be because of a genuine connection, not because I had to, prophecy of the end of the world be damned.

I jumped to my feet, nearly stumbling over myself and into Kaito's lap. He caught me and another jolt of desire swept through my body at his touch. He let go with some visible effort and swallowed. "Lily, don't look at me like that."

"Like what?" I snapped. "Like I just found out that I'm a research project to you? That you just want to fuck me and write about it in some dusty paperwork for your precious Academy?"

Hurt crossed his expression. "No, of course not. What I feel for you isn't contrived. With a bind on you, your powers can't force intimacy that isn't already there, and plus I would never—"

"Enough," I snapped. We'd only just met and I wasn't buying his act. "Just tell me where Dante is. I need to talk to him." This shit with Hendrik was getting out of hand and Kaito had his head so far up his own ass that I wasn't going to get any help from him. Never mind the fact that just being around him made me want to do things that were definitely not student-counselor relationship appropriate.

He folded the paper he'd shown me in half, slowly lining the crease with his thumb. Gods, even that was sexy. "Dante's been sent off-campus on a mission."

I stiffened. "What mission?"

"He wouldn't tell me. He just barged in demanding I keep an eye on you and then he was gone."

"You've been doing a stellar job of keeping an eye on me," I countered. "If I don't show up at Hendrik's place tonight then he's going to hurt Olivia."

Kaito grimaced. "There isn't much I can do about that, but maybe you should go along with it for now. If Hendrik suspects you're from his vision, he won't hurt you. And since you say Hendrik made Dante give a permanent blood sacrifice, my guess would be Dante is up to something dangerous. We need to figure out what it is. Hendrik might have more information."

I leaned back, locking my knees so I didn't sway on my feet. "But I bleed black, Kaito. I can't give Hendrik what he wants, not without revealing what I am." I didn't say it aloud. I was a monster.

He ventured past the tense arousal between us and rested a gentle touch on my hand. "You have a Dark

Mage ally, right? Get her to work a spell that'll make him see what you want him to see. You can give the blood sacrifice without revealing anything if you're careful."

It sounded way too risky.

"Do you hear yourself?" I shrieked. "She only just found out she's a Dark Mage today and she's been through hell. She's exhausted. I can't possibly ask her to do that even if she is capable."

Kaito sighed then swiveled off the desk and kneeled in front of me. "I don't like to use my magic," he muttered, then eased his fingers onto my temples. "I'll make it so you appear to bleed red to anyone who sees you. It'll hold for as long as you want it to." He looked up expectantly.

I swallowed hard. "Okay," I agreed.

His eyes fluttered closed and his mouth parted. I felt something sweep over me, more like an invisible warm blanket than any sort of spell I'd felt so far. It worked its way over my entire body before tightening like elastic wrap. Just when the sensation was starting to get uncomfortable, it faded and he opened his eyes again.

"It's done."

I tilted my head. "So, what are you?" I ventured. "That didn't feel like a spell. I don't think you're a warlock or a Dark Mage."

He smirked. "Observant. No, I'm neither of those things, but what I am is a secret, for now."

Great, more secrets.

I sighed. "So, how do I get Dante to come back?" If he was really out on some dangerous mission, then it definitely had something to do with me, making it my responsibility to make sure he was okay.

Kaito's gaze dropped. "You don't. Dante is a hunter, Lily. This is what he does. He's my friend, I get it. It's hard, but I've come to accept that one day he might go on a mission and he won't be coming back."

Something in me twisted at that thought. I cared what happened to him. Did that mean that Dante was one of my... Virtues? I shoved that thought aside. "Well, thanks for nothing," I snapped. "I'm going to go back to my dorms before I deal with Hendrik. Then I have another exciting day of killing people in the Awakening Arena tomorrow."

He stood and opened the door for me with a gentlemanly stance, which only managed to piss me off more. "Take as much time as you need, Lily. I know this is a lot to take in and I don't expect your supernatural gifts to unfurl all at once. The binds are holding two-thirds of who you are at bay so that you have a chance to bring out the hidden part of you that will be vital in fulfilling this prophecy."

"I don't know if you realize this," I said, snarling the words, "but I don't give two shits about some stupid prophecy. You're not going to put the fate of all the realms on my shoulders, okay? That's not what's happening here. I'm going to figure out who and what I am and then you'll see that there's nothing special between us. I'm just a succubus trying to feed on you. Someone else can save the world and you can go marry them, all right?"

His expressionless features left me with nothing. I wasn't going to change his mind about me by yelling at him, which meant I just had to go through with all of this Awakening Arena bullshit. It didn't change anything. I still didn't know what I was, and whatever Kaito thought I was... it clearly was wrong. I wasn't prophecy material.

I left Kaito's office with a stone in my chest because in spite of everything... a small part of me wondered if he was right.

What if the world was ending... and I was the only one who could stop it?

Yep, I'm doomed.

FOLLOW THE SMELL OF ROSES
AND BLOOD

EMOTIONS HAD ME FRAZZLED AND I DIDN'T want to face Olivia just yet, so I wandered around campus for a few hours until something that resembled dusk settled over the grounds and my legs began to complain from my endless wandering.

Word must have gotten out that I was a pariah because everyone steered clear of me as I walked by, which was just as well. Less hassle for me to deal with.

I knew that I still had to deal with Hendrik, and he hadn't exactly specified a time I had to meet him so I'd make him wait long enough to get pissed off, but I'd still show up before midnight, or whatever passed as midnight around here.

By the time I made it back to the Freshman Dorms I bypassed the worst of Melinda's Mindfreaks without incident. I paused at my door and let out a deep breath. I wondered if Logan would be in there or if Hendrik's spell would break his habit of sleeping in what had been an abandoned bedroom. My heart did a jump at the thought of seeing Logan again.

Did that mean he was a Virtue... too?

Only one way to find out.

I waved my hand over the panel and the door unlatched. I ventured inside and then stopped, stunned at its transformation.

Was this even the same room?

All the dusty sheets were removed and the room had been cleaned within an inch of its life. The chandeliers gleamed, no cobwebs in sight, and dancing purple lights gave the room a mystical glow.

Olivia popped her head out of the bedroom doorway. She had a scarf wrapped around her hair and sweat beaded her brow. "You're back!" she shrieked, and jumped into the living room, waving her arms at the work she'd done. "Ta-da! Isn't this place awesome? It just needed a bit of sprucing up?"

"A bit?" I said, marveling at how beautiful everything was. I ran my fingers over one of the couches and was surprised at the soft fabric that no longer had any must or grime embedded into it. "How did you do all of this?"

She bounced on her toes and I noticed that her purple eyes had taken on a deeper pitch like the other

Dark Mages. "Well, I was practicing some of my magic, it's kind of coming back to me now, and it worked!" She giggled. "It was pretty fun, actually."

I sank into a couch, grateful to have a place I could sit without worrying. "That's cool, Olivia. I'm glad you're coming into your powers." I forced myself to give her a smile. "Does that mean some of your memories are coming back?"

She flinched as if I'd struck her, then she shook off the reaction and sat next to me, curling her legs underneath her. "Yes and no. I've started to remember basic things, like how to use my magic, where it comes from, and what I am, but I can't remember my family or how I found myself on Earth in the first place." She shrugged. "I think that'll come on its own. I'm starting to remember things, so it's a start."

I rested a hand on hers. "You can't expect everything to come back in one day. You've made a lot of progress already."

She smiled. "You're right. I shouldn't be too hard on myself." She let out a long sigh. "It's not so much that, though, that's bothering me... my memories I mean. It's the fact that I know what it means to be a Dark Mage now... like what it *really* means."

I leaned in. "Oh? Is it bad?" I wouldn't think Fortune Academy would have accepted any supernaturals that were inherently evil, yet, Hendrik had a lot of wrongness to him that I could taste on his magic.

She shivered. "So, you know witches and warlocks, right? They're very similar to Dark Mages."

I nodded. "Yeah, okay. Both are magic-users. What about it?"

"Well," she said, biting her lip, "they branched off by the *means* of how they get their powers. The original witches and warlocks made deals with immortal spirits a long time ago and the race was invented. Nowadays some trade their souls to demons to get even more power. But Dark Mages? They're a step beyond that. Dark Mages use their own souls as a source of power, in effect devouring it..." She leaned in, her eyes taking on a gleaming pitch that had a depth to it that made my skin crawl. "What I'm saying is... that I don't have a soul... Lily. It was sacrificed at my birth to give me immortality and a finite source of magic."

I let out a long breath. "Whoa."

"Yeah," she agreed and slumped into the sofa. "Whoa."

"So, all the Dark Mages, Hendrik and the rest, they don't have any souls?"

She nodded and began braiding a few strands of her hair. "Correct, which is why their magic is so strong, but it's not *infinite*. That's where blood duty comes in. They —we... need to feed off of sacrifice in order to fuel spells that cost more than our natural reserves can handle. When multiple Dark Mages are in close proximity, like here at the Academy, it's possible to pool magic together. When I Awakened, I didn't know what I was doing and I might have... stolen a bit of Hendrik's clan magic."

I gripped the side of the sofa, anger building up in me. "So, now you owe a debt," I concluded. Great. Then I straightened. "So in order to fuel the Awakening Arena and the other spells I've seen Hendrik use, people have to suffer?"

"Sacrifice," she agreed, "the shedding of blood."

Well, hopefully that meant that places like the Awakening Arena might be self-sustaining, to an extent.

"That doesn't make me feel any better about having to see him tonight," I admitted, "much less donate to his blood duty." I looked around the room again warily. "How much magic did you expend cleaning this place? I mean, you said you have a finite source and you might be drawing on the clan resources without even realizing it. Should you really be wasting it on frivolous things?" If she was using her own magic, it might be magic she needed to survive. If she was using Hendrik's magic... I was sure he was keeping a close tally.

Not that I didn't appreciate a clean room to come home to, but all of this could have been done by some good old fashioned elbow grease. I didn't want Olivia to expend magic she didn't have, especially not to make my life more comfortable.

Olivia shrugged. "I guess you have a point. I was so excited to remember how to use my magic again that I guess I got a little carried away." She jolted upright. "Oh, that reminds me. I made this too." She dug into her skirt pockets and produced an orb. It reminded me of my demon conjuring orb, but it had a rainbow hue to it. "A few spells came back to me, one of them being how to make a truth orb."

I raised a brow at her. "Truth orb?"

She dangled the object between her fingers before I relented and took it, letting the bauble fall into the palm of my hand. It surprised me by how chilled it was, as if she'd put it in the freezer before giving it to me.

"If you crush this around someone, say... Hendrik, then he'll be forced to tell you the truth. It'll also make him more amenable to suggestion without outright fighting his free will. It can't make him do anything he isn't inclined to do already, but it'll help."

I sighed and tucked the bauble into my skirt pocket. It hissed in a moment of protest as it bumped up against the demon conjuring orb before calming down. I was building quite the collection of magical artifacts. "Well, I appreciate it, but don't use any more of your magic until we understand how it works, all right? We don't know what happens when you run out."

Olivia's face paled, making her dark eyes stand out even more. "Oh, I guess you're right. I hadn't even thought of that." She swallowed hard, then seemed to force on a smile. "Well, ready to go talk to Hendrik? Can't keep the big bad Dark Mage waiting!"

I groaned and rolled onto the edge of the couch. "You're far too chipper. You know he's just going to bully us some more, right?" Ignoring him likely wasn't an option either. He had too much information that we needed. Olivia needed to get her magic under control and I needed to get Dante—and his lost hand—back. Plus, I needed to know about the vision he'd had about me. I needed to know if I was really this fated savior that Kaito saw me as.

Olivia bounced to her feet and offered me a hand. "I'm counting on it, because if I've learned anything about you since we met, it's that you don't let *anybody* push you around." She grinned. "Let's truth bomb this bully."

FORTUNE ACADEMY WAS creepy at night, although the fact that we were going to pay blood duty to a Dark Mage didn't help the ambiance.

"What do you think he'll do?" I asked, starting to

worry about this arrangement. I hadn't tested to see if Kaito's magic had worked on me.

Olivia shrugged. "I don't think it'll be so bad. The other students do blood duty all the time." She nudged me playfully with her shoulder. "You know, I think he just likes you. Big bad mages like Hendrik have better things to do with their time than frighten freshmen."

I doubted that Hendrik was giving me so much attention because he had a crush on me. He was close to figuring out who I was, which both thrilled and terrified me. Hendrik might give me answers that Kaito wouldn't... but at what cost?

WE ARRIVED at the Dark Mage dorms far too quickly for my liking. I was tired from the long day and I wasn't looking forward to dealing with whatever crap Hendrik had in mind for us, but Olivia squeezed my hand and gave me a reassuring smile. I wasn't just doing this for me. Having someone else who deserved my help—or at least rectify the damage I'd caused—gave me enough resolve to wave my hand over the pad next to the door.

A strange beep I hadn't heard before sounded, then a glow blinked above us. Olivia and I looked up.

"A magical security cam?" I wondered.

She tilted her head and sniffed. "Smells like Hendrik's magic. Neat trick."

I took in a long inhale, but I couldn't sense the blood-tinged roses. Before I could ask Olivia what Hendrik's magic smelled like to her, the door jarred open.

I remembered the way to Hendrik's room and I immediately started up the staircase. Olivia followed me. "Uh, you know where to go?"

Oh, right, I wasn't supposed to know which room was Hendrik's.

I shrugged. "Just follow the smell, right?"

She chuckled uneasily as we climbed the steps. There weren't any other Dark Mages out and about. They didn't seem to like to loiter like the girls in my dormitory did.

"Where do you think everyone is?" I asked.

Olivia shrugged. "Probably in their rooms doing Dark Magey things."

I chuckled as we approached Hendrik's door. "Is that the scientific term?"

The door flung open, revealing Hendrik who nearly barreled over us. "Oh," he said, frowning, "figured you'd wait in the lobby." He narrowed his eyes on me. If he was going to ask me how I knew which room was his, he decided against it. Either way, the look on his face said he didn't like being surprised.

Good, I wanted him uneasy.

He held open the door and silently invited us inside. Curiosity bubbled in me and won over the pounding in my heart that said I was going into a lion's den.

"Damn," I breathed. The room was gorgeous and much larger than my "suite" that Dante had found for me. High ceilings made the living room seem like it expanded into the clouds, letting in moonlight through crystal clear skylights. Luxurious furniture surrounded a roaring fireplace and a kitchen lingered in the shadows, spotlighted by two overheads that illuminated a stocked bar. Was alcohol permitted on campus?

Answering my question, Hendrik poured himself a drink, not bothering to ask if either of us wanted one. The golden liquid sloshed as he swirled it, sticking one hand in his pocket as he smirked at us. "Why don't you have a seat," he said, indicating his drink towards the fireplace. "I have some questions before we get started."

He was being way too nice to us. My hackles went up and Olivia stiffened as she shared a glance with me that said she wasn't buying it either. For some reason, Hendrik being nice was even more unnerving than if he'd been threatening our lives.

I felt acutely aware that there weren't any witnesses here and according to Kaito, Hendrik had every right to boss us around. Maybe there was a line he couldn't cross without breaking Academy rules, but how far down the road of sanity that line might be... I didn't want to guess.

Olivia and I took our seats gingerly, opting for separate chairs rather than the loveseat. The chairs would give me more stability if I needed to get to my feet quickly and Olivia seemed to have the same idea as she sat on the edge, setting her feet flat on the ground ready to bolt for the door at any sign of trouble.

Hendrik chuckled at our obvious unease. "Relax. I can be a hard ass, but you've both demonstrated obedience by coming here. I don't kick weaklings when they're down. All I ask for is cooperation, and as long as you continue to give that to me, you have nothing to fear."

Rage boiled in my chest. He thought that he could just order everyone around and he'd get away with it. I clenched my fingers around the chair's armrest and my rune burned on my arm as I resisted the urge to use my succubus powers. I knew what they felt like. I could sense that Hendrik wanted me. It was in the subtle way his gaze lingered on my body and as much as it both excited and revolted me, I could use that to my advantage—but not by revealing what I was. I couldn't give him any leverage against me, so I was going to have to do this the old fashioned way.

It was something Jess had taught me. When a man wanted you, then you played hard to get and you reminded him what he was missing by being a jerk face.

I forced myself to lean back in my chair and crossed my legs, allowing my skirt to ride up my thigh. I didn't reach down to correct it and his gaze lingered on my skin. "Where's Dante?" I pressed while he was distracted.

His midnight gaze flashed to me. "Why do you ask?" He eased onto the edge of the sofa and took a sip of his drink. "If this is about Logan, I just needed to separate him from you. I worked hard for that alliance and I won't have it undone in a single day by a freshman."

"Don't care about your stupid alliances," I said, scratching at my rune that was starting to burn. I was tugging on Hendrik's desire and he leaned instinctually towards me. The heady sense of domination over him made my core tighten. "I know that you chopped off Dante's hand and he thought it would grow back. It didn't. Now he's off-campus on some mission. I want to know where he is."

Hendrik gave me a raised brow. "No wonder my spell was so easy to work. Are you sleeping with the hunter?" Jealousy flickered across his features.

Olivia's chair creaked as she shifted her weight uncomfortably. I'd almost forgotten that she was there.

Hendrik startled, also seeming to have forgotten about my Dark Mage friend. "Let's not dwell on unimportant matters. You're here to pay your blood debt." He set his glass onto the end table and stood, going to the mantle and drawing out a blade from the tiny drawer.

He held it up and the metal flashed unnaturally against the firelight. "Who's first?"

I crossed my arms like I'd seen Jess do, plumping my breasts up to strain against my uniform. Hendrik's eyes went to the distraction. "Thought you said Olivia was off the hook? I was donating in her place, right?"

The Dark Mage rested the point of the dagger against his finger and twirled the hilt in thought. "Maybe I changed my mind and require blood from both of you." He gave me a wicked grin that rivaled Logan's wolfish teeth with raw malice. A different sort of metallic need scented the air and my stomach turned. His arousal heightened at the idea of hurting me, both emotionally and physically. He tore his gaze from me and rested his sights on Olivia. "The new mage should go first."

"No," I said, rushing to my feet. "You're not going to touch her. That's the deal."

His grin faded. "Or what?"

I didn't have time for his shitty games. I pulled out the orb that Olivia had given me and crushed it in my palm.

A terrifying otherworldly screech filled the room and darkness bowed in on us instantly.

Oops.

Wrong orb.

SACRIFICE

So I might have just conjured a demonspawn from hell.

No big deal.

The creature unfurled from raw shadow where black ooze had dropped from my hand onto what had once been a pristine—and likely expensive—carpet.

Hendrik's eyes widened and he grabbed Olivia's arm, shoving her behind him.

Did he just... try to protect her?

The creature's red eyes glowed as it took us in like a newborn emerging from its mother. If... that mother was a pit of shadow and the newborn was a terrifying creature with sharp teeth.

Its gaze latched onto me first and it tilted its head as if curious. It tried to speak to me, but the garbled words that came out of its mouth didn't make any sense.

Hendrik moved so slowly I almost didn't notice when he took the ceremonial dagger and sliced a long line across his palm. My nostrils flared at the pungent scent of roses and blood that hit the air.

Blood magic.

He worked his magic skillfully, weaving it silently as his lips moved and power worked through the air, but it wasn't enough. The demonspawn lost its focus on me and spun on the source of the attack, its sliced nostrils flaring as it bared its teeth and screeched loud enough to make me throw my hands over my ears.

"Keep it in the shadow!" Hendrik barked at me.

The demonspawn lashed out and a claw caught on Hendrik's leg, sending blood splashing across the furniture. He collapsed to one knee, but kept the dagger to his wrist and didn't stop working the powerful spell that had the room flooding with a scent that overpowered the sulfur-sick sweetness of the demonspawn's entry.

I had no fucking idea how to keep the demonspawn in the shadow. It crawled, only a fourth of it still left in the portal as it sought to devour its new target. I instinctually knew that if this thing got free it would wreak havoc on Fortune Academy. Any hope I had of discovering who I was here would end, along with countless lives. I'd made a mistake thinking a demonspawn could be used as a weapon. It was wild and savage. Barely contained hatred and madness ran in fine runes across its chalky skin as it gazed at me, seemingly mesmerized by whatever magic it sensed in my veins.

Deciding that I wasn't worth eating, it turned to Hendrik. I didn't like the expression it wore on its face as a long, pink tongue whipped around its lips in anticipation of a tasty meal.

As much as I disliked Hendrik, something in me had formed a connection, too. A deep sense of understanding came over me as I tasted his magic on the air and deciphered his intentions. He didn't run or try to hide from the danger I'd brought to his home. He would face this abomination and protect what he cared about, even two new students he was trying to teach a lesson. In his own way, he meant well. Being hard on us was his way of helping us step into a supernatural community neither of us really understood.

I probably should have had some miraculous magical revelation and used my innate magic to keep the creature I'd released contained, but I did the first thing that came to mind and I grabbed the creature's hind leg and yanked hard. It whirled on me in protest and slashed out. Blinding pain seared up my ribcage where it'd got me and I stumbled back, gripping onto the burning wound.

Olivia launched from around Hendrik, in spite of his attempt to stop her, and her pitch-black eyes burned with power. Her gifts had been dormant for so long that they burned in her, begging to be used. I also worried that she didn't know her limits. Her powers were too fresh, too eager, and from what she'd told me, if she hit her limit then she was putting her own life in danger.

Regardless of the consequences, Olivia waved her fingers through the air, working and weaving her magic that only had a tasteless sweetness to it like the cold dust of a winter morning. Frost formed on the furniture, creased up the walls, and the demonspawn snarled in outrage as it retreated further into its shadow for warmth.

Well, that was clever. Hell sure would be a lot more warm and toasty than a room encased in ice.

While the demonspawn wouldn't fully regress into the portal, Hendrik's magic came to a crescendo and crashed over the room in a wave. His black eyes took on a red hue and he threw his head back as a surge of power coursed through him as if of its own free will. Magic wrapped around the demonspawn like a giant net, tugging the creature deeper into the shadow until it sank into it, only its head remaining at the top.

The beast tossed one last look of defiance my way and clawed at its prison. It spoke again, this time snarling something that I could only interpret as threats on my life.

There was something else it said, too, that made my

skin crawl. Beady eyes bore a red gaze into me as the creature formed the words slowly and carefully, doing everything it could to make sure I understood.

The language was still foreign to me, but the meaning was clear. The formless words came across the air, climbing over the tapestry of magic that bound it.

You think you're different.

You think you're not a monster.

...You're wrong.

"WHAT THE FUCK WAS THAT?" Hendrik snarled, still bleeding freely on the floor from an impressive gash across his leg and the slice he'd made on his hand. He balled his fingers into a fist to stem the bleeding, but red droplets rolled freely over his knuckles.

Ignoring the ornery Dark Mage that had brought this on himself, I helped Olivia to the sofa and eased her onto it. Her lips were blue and ice coated her fingertips. She trembled and hugged herself as frost puffed from her breath. Her pitch-black eyes had taken on a frosty hue and her cheeks looked as if she'd found glittery blue blush to powder over her skin.

"Are you okay?" I asked her, softly rubbing her arms,

trying to bring life back into her body. She'd overextended her powers for sure and fear pinched my chest.

Her teeth chattered as she tried to talk. "W-Will... be," she promised, then gave me a shaky smile, but she was dangerously weak.

I needed to get her warm. An icy crust had formed over the spot where the demonspawn had been sent back to hell and the fireplace was hopelessly frozen. I glanced between it and Hendrik. "Can you get that burning again?" I asked him.

He scoffed. "Seriously? Have I not expended enough of my magic containing your temper tantrum?"

"I didn't *mean* to summon a demonspawn, okay?" I yelled, lifting my chin in defiance. "Not that you didn't deserve it. You were being an asshole."

He rolled his eyes and staggered to his feet as he limped over to the fireplace. "You both owe me triple blood duty now," he vowed, then allowed some of his blood to drop onto the fireplace.

The ice instantly melted and flames flickered to life, bringing blessed heat into the room. I relaxed and continued to rub at Olivia's arms. "Sorry," I whispered to her with an apologetic smile.

Olivia grinned and eased onto her side, her eyelids growing heavy. "You're full of surprises, aren't you?" As if unable to keep her eyes open anymore, she fluttered them closed and her cheeks took on a more natural rosy hue as warmth finally seeped into her. She drew in a deep breath and then she was asleep.

"She'll survive," Hendrik said, leaning against the mantle as he popped open a first aid kit from behind the wall. Apparently patching up wounds was a regular thing around here. "I couldn't have sent the creature back to hell without her help," he admitted. "Depending on her involvement, perhaps I'll waive her blood duty for now. She seemed surprised that you'd summoned it."

I blinked at him, not sure if I was more surprised to see him pulling out a thread and needle with a bottle of alcohol or the fact that he was showing an ounce of logic. "She had nothing to do with it," I bit off. "I had the conjuring orb that I'd gotten from a friend before I came to the Academy."

Hendrik raised an eyebrow at that. "Impressive, bringing such an artifact on campus grounds without being detected." He thoughtfully peeled away the shredded edge of his uniform pants leg, revealing the nasty gash the demonspawn had given him. He didn't wince at the pain, but diligently cleaned the blood away, wiping the wound with disinfectant before readying his thread and needle. Remembering the demonspawn had gotten a swipe at me, I quickly checked under my shirt, only to find flawless skin. Either healing was a newly manifested ability, or I was imagining things.

Hendrik tried to find a position where he could keep the wound pinched closed and sew up the gash, but it was at an awkward angle and his injured hand couldn't hold the skin taut enough.

I huffed an irritated sigh. "Let me help," I said, snatching the needle from him.

He opened his mouth to protest, but then shut it when I knelt between his thighs. Blood used to make me queasy, but now I just felt desensitized. Even if I didn't have my memories, I had my instincts that were inching closer to the surface, and it made me uneasy of what kind of life I had before the Academy.

Focusing, I positioned the needle at the end of the wound and began stitching.

Hendrik stiffened, wincing as I made the first puncture, but his jaw worked in silence as I sewed up the wound.

"So," I said, threading the needle, "I suppose this was more than you bargained for when you asked us to come here." I glanced up at him to gauge his reaction. I wanted to push him off his high horse and get him to see me as an equal, or at least as less of a freshman he could bully.

He waited until I'd finished the last stitch, knotting the thread neatly, before he spoke. A fine layer of sweat beaded across his forehead. "Have you done this before?" he asked, admiring my work.

I shrugged. "No memories." I pointed to my chest. "Dud, remember?"

He chuckled, his gorgeous smile transforming his face in ways that made me want to let my guard down. "You could have fooled me."

I became acutely aware that I was still in-between his legs and, in a sense, we were very much alone. Olivia slept soundly on the couch, the fire slowly bringing warmth back into her chilled body, and a new kind of warmth crept up my own thighs when I turned back to the handsome Dark Mage who was still smiling at me. "What?" I snapped. "Thought you were pissed off at me."

"Oh I am," he promised. His hand rested on my shoulder and his fingers ground into my collarbone in a possessive way, "but I'm also impressed, you—"

His words cut off as his pitch-black eyes swirled with a glimmer of magic, reacting to something inside of... me.

Touch seemed to amplify my suppressed gifts and even though I couldn't draw on his life-force like the succubus in me wanted to, I could still taste his desire for me. He liked a woman that was on the dangerous side, unpredictable, and a mystery. I was all of those things in a neat and tidy box as if I'd wrapped myself as a present left on his doorstep.

There was something else in his gaze that had me on

edge. His desire for me left a sweet taste in my mouth, but he had his own magic as well that crawled over me at our contact. It recognized me.

"I've seen you before," he said, his voice low with accusation. "You're..."

"Nope," I said, launching to my feet. I stepped out of his reach and broke the contact, snapping free of his magic that had been tasting me and threatening to burrow under my skin. My runes burned hot, although, thankfully, they were still invisible. I stuffed my hands into my pockets and glowered at the Dark Mage. "You've lost a lot of blood," I reminded him. "We never met before I came to the Academy." I crushed the remaining orb as I said the words, making a puff of magic filter through the room.

Hendrik didn't seem to notice, and instead he relaxed under the compulsion of the spell. He *wanted* to believe that I wasn't the girl from his vision. He wanted to see me as a freshman at his academy where he was in charge. That was something familiar, something he could control.

If I was the girl from his vision...

No, he couldn't fathom it. My spell made sure of that. It capitalized on a deep-seated fear of what it might mean to him if I really was meant to head off the Third Echo of Calamity and I'd come to him for support. He had a cushy deal here at Fortune Academy and he had plans that would help his people, although I couldn't see deep enough into his black heart to decipher what those plans were. All I could glean was that I was not a part of those plans and Hendrik, the all mighty leader of the Dark Mage clan, had enough responsibility on his plate without adding the fate of the world onto it.

"You're right," he said, shaking his head and rubbing his temples. With a grunt, he tried to stand and put weight on his injured leg. He stumbled back against the mantle and hissed with pain. "Well, let's get down to business then," he said, resolve seeming to wash over him as he transformed back into his old asshole self. His midnight eyes flashed up to meet mine and any kindness I'd seen there had vanished. Maybe my compulsion spell had worked a little too well to push him away and convince him that I wasn't anyone special. "Any new Dark Mage that comes into my clan owes a blood debt." He glanced at my sleeping friend. "She's in no condition to provide it. In fact, she's drawn so much magic from her reserves that she'll die if she tries to work a spell again without entering into our collective and drawing from the blood sacrifices." His jaw worked with irritation as he faced me again. "Dark Mages don't tap out on my watch, not in my clan. You will repay what she owed, what she took, and what she'll need to survive. Those are my conditions."

I stared at him in surprise. I'd been under the

impression that the blood sacrifice he demanded was some power struggle, but he had a legitimate purpose for it. His clan survived on shared magic and worked together to make sure not any one mage's reserves dropped too far. Hendrik could have drawn on his collective for the magic he needed to banish the demon-spawn, but he'd used his own suffering to power the spell. "Well, why didn't you just put it that way in the first place?" I asked, allowing irritation to creep into my voice. "I thought you just wanted to boss us around."

He staggered towards the kitchen, taking his empty whisky glass with him. "I'm a leader. Bossing idiots around is what I do and I don't need to explain myself."

Letting that insult slide by, I followed him as he collected a half-empty bottle and poured golden liquid into the glass. He swirled it around before downing the whole thing in one gulp.

I glowered at him. He was making me wait on purpose. "I came here because you know where Dante is, and you took something from him," I said, trying to pick my words carefully. When he turned to glare at me, I stiffened. "His hand hasn't grown back. Apparently it usually does."

Hendrik poured another glass before raising it to his lips. This time he sipped leisurely at the contents. "The magic the hunter needed required a permanent sacrifice.

It'll take double the power to restore him, if that's what you want."

"Just tell me what to do," I said without hesitation. Whatever Dante was up to, I knew it was because of me. I would fix this for him.

Hendrik raised an eyebrow. "You're already in enough debt to me as it is," he reminded me. He set his glass down and began counting off on his fingers. "Let's see, enough blood to pay for a fledgling Dark Mage, which might have been impossible to take from you without any permanent damage, but now," he *tsked* and counted off on another finger, "you also took three weeks of my own magic to banish the demonspawn you so carelessly summoned. Not to mention the damage to my own body." He tested his weight on his leg and grunted. "My wounds will have to heal naturally, slowly, unless you provide the sacrifice needed to heal. I don't want to take any further resources from my clan."

I wasn't sure where I was going to get enough sacrifice to cover that sort of debt, but I'd figure it out. "Like I said," I said, digging my fingers into my arms, "just tell me what to do and it'll be done."

I didn't like the grin that stretched across his handsome features, turning them sinister. "I have a few ideas, but you're not going to like it."

I shifted my weight onto my hip. "Well, go on, I'm listening."

He sipped at his whisky again, delight crinkling his eyes as his gaze raked over me again. He smacked his lips with satisfaction. "Well, my allies have plenty of power they don't always know how to part with. There's Orion. His weakness is sex. Take that away from him for a period of time and that'll cover at least a third of the sacrifice you need to recover your debt."

I snorted on a laugh. "Really? Making a demigod abstain from sex is some great sacrifice?"

He nodded, gravely serious. "Greek myths hold a lot of truth to them. The gods divine their power released from sex and pleasure. It's similar to the succubi, but they don't feed on a person's life-force that's made vulnerable by passion. They're able to extract the raw power from passion itself, like I am able to extract power from pain."

I shrugged. "Okay, make Orion hang up his dick wand for a while, I can do that." No fucking clue how I was going to get Orion to stop sleeping around—he was literally a playboy demigod—but I'd cross that bridge when I got to it. "So, what else?'

"Then there's Logan," Hendrik said wistfully as he eased onto a stool, only wincing slightly as he twisted his leg into a more comfortable position, revealing an attractive curve on the inside of his thigh that the succubus in me wanted to explore. "He already suffers, but I haven't figured out a way to get his defenses down enough to capture that raw energy. He's a lone wolf, you see, yet he's bound to lead his pack. He's an alpha, even if he never wanted to be." Hendrik pointed at me. "Get him to turn on his pack and it'll break those defenses."

"I thought you wanted me to stay away from Logan," I sneered. "Now you want me to break him?"

Hendrik chuckled. "Break his defenses, that's all. Logan will be fine, and maybe better off in the end."

The thought of hurting Logan made my stomach twist, but if what Hendrik said was true and Logan didn't want to be alpha of his pack, he was right, I could be helping him in the long run. "Okay," I relented. "I'll see what I can do."

"Wonderful," Hendrik said, beaming. He eased to his feet and beckoned me to follow. "You'll need an artifact to absorb the suffering. I have just the thing."

I followed Hendrik into his bedroom which was easily three times the size of my shared room with Olivia. He gripped a painting that could only be described as the underworld decorated by elaborate caverns and pits of fire, and pulled it away from the wall. It twisted on hinges, revealing a safe.

He leaned down and a scanner moved over his eyes. I wondered how pitch-black eyes could have a signature, but the safe seemed to recognize him and popped open.

I tried to see around his shoulder, but he blocked my view of the contents. He pulled something out and then shut the safe and painting again, settling both back with a *click*.

He presented a necklace with a stunning red gem dangling on the end of it. "A Blood Stone," he announced with pride. "I save it only for special occasions, but in this case, I believe you'll put it to good use."

He took my hand and dropped the gem into it, the silver chain pooling on my palm in a fine swirl. I examined it, trying not to be too impressed with how beautiful it was, but the ruby hue was so deep and the facets of the gem caught the light in a way that had me mesmerized. I tore my gaze away from it and raised a brow at him. "How does it work?"

He closed my fingers around the prize and flashed me a smile. "Just be the cause of the sacrifice. The stone will do the rest." He waved his hand over mine and a trickle of magic settled into the chain, heating up slightly before cooling again. "Wear it, don't take it off. When the job is done, come back to me." He winked. "I might even let you keep it after I extract your debt."

It felt appropriate that the first piece of jewelry I'd ever gotten from a guy would be a Dark Mage artifact designed to feed on suffering.

I nodded, pinching my lips together as I accepted his proposal. If he meant to let me keep the stone, then this wouldn't be the only job I'd be doing for him.

He eased his arm around my shoulder and guided me

out of his bedroom, far too pleased with himself. "I believe this is a start of a wonderful alliance," he said with a grin.

The scent of roses and blood followed us out and I wondered what kind of shit I'd gotten myself into now.

WATCHING OLIVIA SET UP HER NEW CLASS schedule after three weeks of waiting had me feeling a bit envious. It was school policy to enforce an adjustment period and Olivia was ready to crawl out of her own skin and get started. We'd been on the same page until now, forming a routine that involved going out to eat and Olivia patching me up after my bouts at the Awakening Arena.

But now... it was time for her to move on without me.

Olivia spread out all the courses available onto a table and admired the different routes her life could take. Unlike witches who were bound to a coven, Dark Mages could specialize their magic and had enough freedom to contribute to the clan rather than draw from its source. Hendrik might have gone the traditional route of harnessing pain into power, but so many other elements could provide energy. I eyed the titles with curiosity, wondering if Olivia would be interested in sorcery that focused on nature or astrology.

Thinking of astrology made me think of Orion... and I grimaced.

Olivia pointed to one of the papers. "What do you think about this one?" She pursed her lips. "Introduction to Alchemy. According to the description, energies exist in all elements and this provides a fundamental understanding that requires three textbooks. It sounds like it's just a lot of reading, and maybe something I could do without expending magic, doesn't it?"

Olivia had been trying to find classes where she wouldn't have to use magic at all, which was a challenge for a fledgling Dark Mage. It was going to take some time to pay back the debt we owed Hendrik. He'd made it very clear that if she used her magic, even for a small spell, her life would be in grave danger. Her body continually struggled to find energy to fuel her new magic and the clan rejected her attempts to draw more power from the collective than she was putting in.

Olivia was so eager to figure out who she was that I could tell it was killing her not being able to go all-out. Even though I could relate to her ambition were I in the same position, I knew we had to do this the right way.

First I had to fix the damage I'd caused and then we could both figure out who we were, together.

I peered over her shoulder at the alchemy class card description. "Sounds like a great class," I said and gave her a warm smile. "Do you know what the professor's like?"

"Oh," she said, drawing back from the table, "I hadn't considered the professors. I'm going to have to rearrange all of the cards."

I nodded in agreement. After a couple of weeks at the Academy and no sign of improvement from the Awakening Arena, Miss Williams had reluctantly given me a couple of classes to keep me occupied. I found how useful those classes were depended entirely on the professor. Even the teachers had alliances and it became quickly obvious who was in league with either Hendrik, Melinda's Mindfreaks, the Demis, or the Shifters.

"I don't know about the professor who teaches Alchemy," Olivia went on. "Who do you think I could ask? Maybe some of the Dark Mages?"

Even though we had our own small alliance, neither of us knew much about the inner social workings of the campus other than what we gleaned for ourselves, which wasn't much. Being a dud made it hard to build any sort of alliance and Logan hadn't talked to me ever since our fall-out. Olivia was more than understanding. She didn't press me every time I came back from the Awakening

Arena ashen and defeated. No one was able to kill me. Without the true fear of death, my instincts refused to come out and the truth about who I was remained buried somewhere deep inside of me. In spite of my pretty face and my fragile appearance, I was a lot harder to fight than I looked. Olivia told me I should be proud of my skills, but it made me even more concerned about what kind of life I had before I'd found myself drenched in blood at Monster Mother's door.

"I don't know if it's a good idea to talk to the other Dark Mages, not yet," I said half-heartedly. "They know I'm Hendrik's little bitch right now." I fingered the stone around my neck that felt more and more like a collar that leashed me to Hendrik's clan. In spite of that, I felt a fondness towards the gem I couldn't describe. It awarded me curious stares on campus, but it was too big to tuck under my uniform.

For now, I'd play along until I found a way to get Hendrik off my ass.

Olivia went back to sorting out the course cards, aligning them based on the professors she knew about and those she didn't. "I heard this one hates mages," she grumbled, tossing it to the floor. "Oh and this one hates women." By the end of her sorting, she'd eliminated almost half her pile.

I didn't have the luxury of picking out new classes. Other than fighting at the Awakening Arena and taking on a couple of basic classes like supernatural history and parallel world realm studies, I knew what I had to do.

It was time for me to plot out my first payment to Hendrik's Blood Stone.

Orion.

I'd been racking my brain on how to get Orion to do what I needed. He might be a demigod, but surely he had a weakness. Three weeks of stalking him still didn't give me much to go on. All the Demis seemed to do was host orgies. I still wasn't sure how I felt about peeking into the Demi Dormitories only to find Orion in the middle of a pile of bodies, his elegant form trapped in the middle of a tangle of arms and legs. The succubus in me always reacted and made me feel a bit ashamed, but I needed to understand how his powers worked.

The Demis fed on the other students, but not in a way that qualified them for Monster Academy. They didn't take magic that fueled life-force, but rather the demigods were like mages on steroids. They converted pleasure into power. If anything, the students who came out of the Demi Dorms seemed rejuvenated and had a glow bubbling up just underneath their skin that seemed to last for days. If fucking a demigod really did give a power boost, it was easier to understand why so many were willing to partake in the orgies.

Building up my courage to venture out again, I got up from my chair and stretched. "I think I'll go for a walk," I told Olivia. The Demis were due for another orgy right about now. If anything, they were like clockwork and predictable when it came to their feeds.

Olivia, still glued to her remaining class cards, waved absently at me. "Don't get into any trouble," she called out.

Me, get into trouble? Can't imagine what would give her that idea.

With dusk fast approaching the campus, only the shifters and a few Dark Mages were out tonight. The Mindfreaks liked to hole up early.

I still wasn't used to the alternate world I was starting to call home—a temporary home where everyone hated me. The black and blue sky seemed bruised, as if it had been the one trapped in the Awakening Arena instead of me. There was no sun or moon to speak of, just an endless sea of murky color that had me feeling claustrophobic. I wasn't sure what had happened to the two moons I'd seen my first night at the Academy, but they were long gone now, replaced by a vast expanse of nothingness. I craved some celestial object to ground me, give me direction and focus on an otherwise endless night.

Ironic that I would be seeking out a demigod named Orion.

I came upon the Demi Dorms and stopped short of crossing the sidewalk where the ground took on a golden hue. It was as if the entire building was made of gold and brass and the metallic beauty bled into the streets. If the orgies really contributed to the demigods' power, then it made more sense why the building had such a celestial glow to it.

Curling my fingers around my necklace, I crossed the boundary and went straight for the front door.

I rapped my knuckles on the sturdy frame and waited. There was no touchpad for entry to the Demi Dorms. The building itself seemed to have a sentience of its own and I felt like it always knew I was watching when I came around to spy on Orion and his friends.

The door flung open and Ally, Daughter of Athena, gave me a low whistle. "Well look who it is, the dud." She beamed. "Come on in. We've been waiting for you." She turned on her heel, sending her braids flinging over her shoulder, as she marched inside and left the door open for me.

I'd only gotten to see some of the massive rooms on the ground floor where most of the orgies were hosted, but the entranceway was even more impressive. I stepped into a brilliance of golden light that fluttered at my steps, sending a cascade of light reeling along the walls as if I'd disturbed a quiet paradise. I followed Ally down the halls with a sense of growing wonder.

Any sense of peace the beauty of the Demi Dorms might have given me was banished when I heard the sensual moans. The magical essence of sexual desire hit me in the chest and I gripped my invisible rune that burned and suppressed my instinct to feed on the life-force it was linked to.

As if Ally sensed a disturbance, she paused and quirked an eyebrow at me. "You did come here for the orgy, right?"

I felt like I should have been insulted by the casual way she asked me that, but it was the truth. I had come here for the orgy.

Not that I was going to participate.

Maybe.

I gave Ally a shaky nod. "Yeah, uh, just nervous. You know, first time."

She glanced down at the Blood Stone I was still touching and I let go of it. She frowned. "You better not be up to something for Hendrik. That won't end well for you."

With that simple threat, she opened the doors to the orgy room and my knees buckled with the wave of sensual and divine power. Low-hanging drapes framed the ceiling and seemed to keep in a cloud of the fog of energy exuded by the students who were in various stages of peeling off their uniforms. I swallowed hard when I spotted Orion in the center, his lips on a woman's neck and his hand running up her thigh. Golden light flickered from every spot he touched her and when he pulled away, he drew in the power in one long breath, his eyes flashing was satisfaction.

Ally took my hand and smiled. "He won't be too busy for you. Come on." She guided me through the tangle of bodies, deftly stepping over limbs and couples interlocked with one another.

Orion eased the half-naked girl onto his lap when he spotted our approach. The grin on his face made me want to punch something. He looked like the cat who'd eaten the canary. "Well, if it isn't our little dud. Did you finally figure out what you were good for? Just a good fuck, right?"

Ally gave me a smirk. "Her roommate owes quite the debt to Hendrik. I'd be wary, Orion."

Orion grinned at me. He wore a simple groin cloth that did little to hide his erection and he patted his well-muscled thigh. "I'm not afraid. Why don't you join me right over here? I could use something new to add to my power." The girl on his other leg shifted closer to him and ran a hand down his chest. She didn't seem insulted as she nibbled on his ear, licking away golden droplets and shivering as the substance grazed her tongue.

"What is that?" I asked, unable to hide my fascination. I was part succubus, after all, so it could come in handy to understand this twist on my own magic that made Orion so powerful.

I'd made the mistake of venturing close enough to be within Orion's reach and he grabbed my fingers, running them over his lips. I flinched away, but then looked down to see the golden powder glimmering on my skin.

"Taste it," he dared me with a wicked smile. His golden eyes flashed with challenge. "Find out for yourself."

I went to wipe my fingers on my uniform, but Ally grabbed my wrist and forced my hand to my mouth. "There, be a good girl," she said as I fought against her. She grinned. "One little taste and you'll be our pet instead of Hendrik's..."

The bitch!

I delved into my supernatural strength to fend Ally off, but she *was* born of the goddess of war. Even I wasn't able to overcome her as she forced the tip of my finger past my lips and rubbed the golden smear across my teeth.

Sweetness exploded in my mouth as the tiny specs of power found their way into my system. I didn't just react to the influx of power Orion had given me, but something in his essence reacted with my own.

Something that gave me power over *him* and not the other way around.

I latched onto that sensation and ground my teeth together, determined not to lose myself to the compulsion running through me that wanted to push that girl off Orion's lap and straddle him right here in front of everyone.

An internal battle worked through me as heat washed over my skin and sensations built between my thighs that made an embarrassing groan come from my mouth. Orion must have misunderstood, because his touch ran up my ribcage and he murmured, "That's right, little pet. Give yourself to me."

My eyes flashed open. "Fuck you!" I spat, then added, "And not in the way you want!"

Orion balked in surprise and Ally was too stunned to do anything but stare at me. Orion had made a mistake giving me power. Even if I didn't know who or what I was, the instinct inside of me that countless bouts at the Awakening Arena couldn't touch erupted into being. I gripped onto the girl who was still licking Orion's ear. "You don't want him," I insisted and a flux of compulsion swept through me and into her body. She flinched, then went rigid as golden liquid seeped off of her like oil against water. She slipped off Orion's lap and rubbed her temples as if dazed. "What am I doing here?" she murmured, then seemed to realize her uniform shirt was completely open. She buttoned it up and gave me an apologetic smile. "Sorry, uh, I think I'm in the wrong place." She stumbled over the field of bodies and with each wave of power that rang out at her footsteps, more of the students flinched and came out of their trances.

"What are you doing?" Orion barked, but it was too late.

The party was over.

I stabbed a finger into his chest, this time steeling myself against the flux of his golden light he tried to push over me. I knew what he tasted like now and he was *mine*. "You think you're so powerful," I sneered. "You think you can bully girls into sleeping with you just because you're a demigod? Well, you're wrong. I've had to walk around knowing what it feels like to be mortal and now it's your turn. No one is going to want to have sex with you, not in the way you're used to. You're going to have to work for it like everybody else." I sealed the words with magical promise, interlacing the command with Orion's essence and making it truth.

Orion launched to his feet, his erection still impressive underneath his groin cloth. Now that I was in control, I tilted my head and admired him with a wry grin. Who was whose pet now?

"Hey, get back here!" Orion barked at the girl. He couldn't even use her name—probably didn't even know it.

The student didn't even give him a backwards glance as she turned the corner and ventured out of sight.

"What the fuck did you just do?" Ally asked, backing away from me with a sense of hesitation in her eyes that said I'd done something worthy to be afraid of.

I shrugged. "Guess you'll have to figure it out."

The students broke from their spell and started putting their clothes back on. Satisfied, I marched through them and out of the Demi Dorms.

When I looked down at my necklace, it gleamed just a little bit brighter.

AWAKENED

OLIVIA AND I WALKED THE HALLS ON THE WAY to our shared class with our arms interlinked and I'd never felt so free in all my life. It was the first time I'd bested someone like Orion who was trying to overpower me all on my own, and even though I'd been helping Hendrik in the process, it felt good. If I could stop Orion, a demigod, from controlling me, then there was hope I could face all of my bullies and come out on top.

"I can't believe you really messed with the Demis like that," Olivia said, elated with the destruction I'd caused. "They'll think twice about messing with our alliance now." She held up a little fist of defiance, making me giggle.

I wrapped my fingers around hers and made her put her hand down. The other students gave us a wide berth and were now giving us frightened stares.

"Don't get too cocky," I warned her. "I'm sure they'll be fighting back."

I still didn't know exactly what I'd done to cock-block the Demis, but all the students seemed aware of the demigods now and that by partaking in any orgy parties, they only made the Demis stronger.

A group of students rushed past, one of them snagging me by the shoulder and whispering, "Orion is on the warpath! You'd better get out of here!"

The fear in the boy's eyes gave me hesitation, but then his gaze flashed to the end of the hall, making him stiffen before he ran away from me so fast I wondered if I'd imagined him.

"You're dumb enough to show your face in class?" Orion spat.

I was used to seeing him with a couple of girls hanging off his arms, which now I knew gave him steady doses of power, but not today. Today Trevor and Zero, the other two male Demis, stood one step behind Orion and glared at me.

"We had a good thing going," Trevor said mournfully, taking out a bottle of water. He unscrewed the lid and started chugging it.

Zero rolled his eyes. "Do you see what you did Orion? The son of Poseidon reduced to water bottles. It's pathetic."

Orion ignored the demigod and zoomed in on me.

He approached and loomed over Olivia and me. My best friend stood her ground and straightened.

"Are you interested in joining our alliance?" Olivia asked. Her voice didn't even waver.

Orion barked a laugh. "Hell no. I'm going to figure out what little spell Hendrik gave you that could have that kind of power." He sniffed at Olivia. "It's certainly not you. Your power's so dried up it's a miracle you're still walking."

Olivia turned her nose up at him. "Whatever." She tugged on my arm. "Come on, Lils. We've got a class to get to."

I wanted to go with her, but something in my Blood Stone was reacting to Orion's negative energy. Heat burned along the chain as it soaked up his rage and suffering. I needed to stay in his vicinity to gather the power I owed Hendrik to restore Olivia and get the Dark Mages off our case. "I'll be right there," I promised her with a reassuring smile.

She hesitated, but then untangled her arm from mine and gave me a wave. "If you need me just call out, okay? Don't take too long." She gave Orion and the other demigods a warning glare before she ventured down the hall.

Orion stepped closer to me and the Blood Stone around my neck burned with an influx of heat. It glowed, but Orion didn't seem to notice. His gaze was fixed entirely on mine as he stared down at me, making me feel small. "You must be a Demi," he said, lowering his voice with accusation. He narrowed his eyes, but I noted that without his constant feed of power the golden light had dimmed, revealing the striking grey shades underneath. "Who's your divine parent? Is it Loki?" He gripped my arm hard enough to make my muscles ache. "Only Loki's offspring could fuck with the Demis like this. Just wait for parent-teacher conferences. You think hiding behind the Awakening Arena can prevent the Dean from calling him? Fucking think again."

I couldn't help but bubble out a laugh. Me? Daughter of Loki? I wish that's what was wrong with me. I knew that whatever I was, it wasn't something easily explained away.

"Why are you laughing?" he snarled and shook me.

I twisted out of his grip, which only seemed to piss him off more. My supernatural strength matched his now that he wasn't being constantly juiced up. "I'm laughing because Loki's going to be really pissed off when he finds out you're blaming him. I'm not a Demi, Orion. I'm not what you think."

His shoulders rolled back. "Yeah, well I'll figure you out."

"Why?" I shot back. I had more than enough of his suffering fueling the Blood Stone resting on my chest that it burned. I was ready to move on from Orion and to my next target, but it was more than that. I could feel his suffering and his frustration like a knot in my chest. I was just as confused and fascinated as he was. "Why do you need magic to get laid?" I pressed. I couldn't help myself and ran my fingers over the thin layer of his shirt, folding my fingers under his tie. He was so fucking gorgeous that he should have no trouble finding a girl interested in him, magical allure or not.

His nostrils flared and he worked his jaw as if my touch stirred something within him. "You don't even know what you did to me, do you?" His voice came out low and with a dangerous growl that made me both excited and a little bit terrified.

I searched his face, trying to understand the expression that had settled there. Hurt crossed his gold-flecked eyes. "Tell me," I said, asking this time. I didn't push any magical compulsion into the question.

Orion's hand reached up to cup my own and he surprised me with the gentleness of his touch. He rubbed his fingers once over my knuckles. "I can't feed on anyone else because I don't *want* anyone else." He lowered, his lips brushing my cheek and making a foreign shiver run through my body. "I want you, Lily Fallen."

This time, I believed him. This wasn't the same cocky demigod who slept with a hundred girls and didn't even know their names. I had a hundred percent of his attention and his body screamed for me. I would have blamed my succubus powers for the effect I had on him, but the rune was quiet on my arm, proving that I wasn't trying to feed on the desire that was wafting off of him. Something else inside of me held onto a connection that marked Orion as mine... and me as his.

Fuck, Orion was one of my Virtues... Wasn't he? A guardian who would help me face the Third Echo of Calamity and save the world.

Damn Kaito and his hot Asian ass being right.

Orion leaned down to kiss me, his lips tender as they claimed mine with sweet possession.

I didn't pull away.

OLIVIA DIDN'T GET a chance to ask me what I had discussed with Orion. The teacher barreled into the topic of humanity's discovery of the supernatural and how we would eventually interact with the non-supernatural when we left Fortune Academy. This was a freshman class for good reason. By "leave the Academy" she didn't necessarily mean graduate.

"Some of you will return to Earth sooner than others," she said with a frown in my direction. "We have study centers across five global cities that can get you a job and integrated safely into society."

A few of the classmates snickered, making me cross my arms and lean back in my chair with my chin stuck up in defiance. No way I was going to be "safely" integrated into anything. The only thing I was integrating with was my destiny to stop the Third Echo of Calamity —assuming I could get my Virtues to stop trying to control me and work with me.

"Miss Fallen," she said when the class was over, earning a surprised glance from me.

"Yes?"

She handed me a slip of paper. "You have one more class added to your docket today. It's in ten minutes."

I unfurled the note with a frown and then hissed. "This is by the Awakening Arena and that's definitely more than a ten-minute walk!"

She shrugged. "Guess you'd better hurry then."

Cursing, I grabbed my bag which thankfully had a few bandages stuffed in the bottom. If this was a surprise Arena run then I was going to need them.

Olivia brushed my arm just before I hurried out. "What is it?" she asked, her pitch-black eyes wide with concern. They'd taken on a foggy texture, like a dog that was too old, and I knew we didn't have much time to rekindle her magic before she started feeling the effects.

I held up my paper for her to see. "New class, apparently." I stuffed the note in my skirt pocket and sighed.

"Going to have to use my super strength to make this one on time. See you later?"

She nodded. "Yeah, okay. Just be careful."

"Always," I promised, giving her shoulder a squeeze before I bolted out of the classroom.

This time of day the campus was way too packed for a full-out run for class, but I didn't have much choice. My professors liked to surprise me and see if I'd fail a new challenge. I wasn't going to give anyone a reason to put me in a study center. I needed to stay at Fortune Academy and figure out who and what I was. I felt like I was so close and if what Kaito believed about me to be true, then it was up to me to prevent the end of the world. No pressure.

I shoved past a Mindfreak bitch who screeched as I barreled by. "Watch it!" she yelled after me.

A snap of magic hit the back of my legs where she tried to compel me to trip, but the command bounced right off of me and ricocheted into a nearby shifter pack of panthers in their human form. Mewls sounded as one of the girls tripped over her own feet.

I wanted to turn back around and teach that Mindfreak to mind her own manners, but I didn't have time. I had bigger supernatural fish to fry.

I made it into class just as a buzzer sounded and the door hissed closed with an audible *click*. I blinked at it and tested the doorknob. Yep, locked. That wasn't a good sign.

"Lily Fallen. Glad you could join us," came the cool voice of a professor that sounded oddly... familiar.

I turned to find four students kneeling on the floor, each with a vial in hand and the professor looming over them.

The professor was none other than Kaito himself. What the fuck was he up to?

If I didn't have my powers, I would have thought Kaito a stranger. He gave me a once-over with complete professional decorum, his silver streak in his hair perfectly in place, but I felt the lust between us just hovering underneath the surface. I wanted to mess up his hair and all it would take was one touch to set those flames alight again and he'd be mine.

As if he sensed my thoughts, he narrowed his eyes and pointed to the last open spot on the floor.

Right, behaving. I can do that.

I gave Kaito a healthy glare in return, because he knew very well that he'd made me rush all the way across campus just to get here and he'd better have a damn good reason to make me jump through hoops.

"All of you are here because you've struggled to awaken your supernatural gifts," he said, pacing in front of us. He brought me a vial like the other students were holding.

I took it and turned it sideways, grimacing as the black liquid inside sloshed slowly to the side.

"This is an experimental class," he continued, marching away from me. "You are the lucky chosen few to get this last chance before more drastic measures are taken. Usually students who do not respond to the Awakening Arena are taken to the Monster Arena." He turned, as if for dramatic effect. "Also known as the West Wing."

I rolled my eyes.

The other students didn't seem as amused by Kaito's demonstration. He was trying to scare me, but it wasn't working. If he really wanted to frighten me he should have had someone else teach the class. Kaito had far too much invested in me for me to fear for my well-being enough to bring out my supernatural instincts, much less fear for my life.

Kaito clapped his hands and the students startled. "Drink your vials. You will be taken into a trance and there you will face your worst fears. You won't be in mortal danger, but your mind won't know the difference."

Oh.

The students stared down at their vials. One girl popped off the cork and tossed the contents back with a determined grimace. We all watched her as she slowly closed her eyes and went still. The air around us popped and the girl's skin took on a grey sheen.

"All of you now," Kaito said, no emotion in his voice at all.

I swallowed hard and looked back at the vial. What was in this stuff? Would I react badly to it? My body liked to fend off any dangerous magical interventions, but Kaito had said that this wouldn't be dangerous. It would just feel dangerous, so my defenses might not try to fend it off until I was already in the trance.

I hesitated long enough for the other students to have taken their vial and go into similar statue-like trances. Kaito kneeled and gave me a weak smile. "I'm sorry to trick you here, but the Dean didn't give me much time." He lifted my hand and popped the cork off the vial. "You know I wouldn't do anything to put you in danger. You can trust me."

Our connection electrified between us from the mere graze of his touch and I sucked in a breath. I ran my finger up the left side of his cheek, following his tattoo into the silver streak of his hairline. He leaned into it, then flinched away. "I know you wouldn't hurt me," I admitted. As much as I wanted to believe that everyone had a secret agenda, Kaito was one of my Virtues. His soul was slowly intertwining with mine... I could *feel* it and my heart ached, wanting to explore more of him. I needed to know his hopes, dreams, and I needed him to know me.

"Then take the vial," he said, lifting it to my lips. "This is how I can help you."

I pushed it away. "Are you sure? My instincts won't come out if I'm really not in danger. I can't be so easily fooled." Melinda had tried her mind tricks on me, as well as many students at Fortune Academy. I didn't see how some black goo would work either.

He nodded. "I'm sure. Please, just trust me."

Sighing, I relented. I still didn't believe him, but I did trust him, so I parted my lips and allowed him to tilt the contents into my mouth.

I expected the black liquid to taste as vile as it looked, but it eased into my system like a fine wine and filled my senses with nostalgic memories that wouldn't quite come to the surface. I fluttered my eyes closed and let the sensation wash over me as I sighed.

"That's it," Kaito said, his voice sounding distant now, "let it guide you home."

Home. I didn't know where that was, but with the magic coursing through me, I had a feeling that before I'd lost my memories, before I'd come to Earth, home felt like this.

WHEN I OPENED my eyes again I was in a world of pitch blackness, but I wasn't afraid. I was familiar with this darkness. A low hum surrounded me with a steady thump as if I was in my mother's womb.

I stretched out my fingers and grazed the thick blackness that encased me. This was home. I could remember it now, before I found myself on Earth. Before I was Lily Fallen.

I was Lilith.

Panic took hold as the memory came back to me. I wasn't home, I was trapped in the Incubus King's basement, trapped in darkness where he hoped I would rot away and die. I wasn't the daughter he'd hoped for.

My mother... she would save me. But how?

I ran through the darkness and hit something hard. I beat my fists against it and screamed. Trapped. I couldn't die. I was an immortal of unnatural proportions.

I was a demonspawn.

This was the other third of my evil heritage that I'd been suppressing. The place where I'd come from before Earth had been hell itself.

Hunger laced through me with such violent pain that I doubled over and cried out. No, this couldn't be true. This couldn't be happening. My worst fear was being a monster and now it was revealed that I was the worst monster of all.

When I went to wipe the tears from my face my

fingers scraped across hard skin and my stomach dropped. Sharp fangs poked from my teeth and I knew that I wasn't the pretty face everyone saw me as in Fortune Academy. This was what I really looked like underneath.

The rune across my arm burned hot, retaliating as if denying that this was my true form. Fresh pain laced through me and I curled up in a ball, for the first time feeling like I was going to die, not because I was trapped in a memory, but because of what I was. I deserved to die. I deserved for Dante to find me right now and plunge a dagger in my chest like he'd done to Jess.

That was all my instincts needed.

I wasn't just a creature from hell. There was something more... something pure. That supernatural part of me awakened and billowed a wave of light through the darkness, banishing my fears and nightmares with searing determination. A heavy weight settled on my back and a soft draping sensation fell over me. I pressed my fingers to my face again, finding the skin smooth, the fangs gone.

What the hell was I?

EPILOGUE

WHEN I CAME BACK TO THE REAL WORLD, I wasn't in the classroom anymore. No students, no empty vials, just a soft bed and Kaito leaning over me, his eyes alight with concern and that silver streak in his hair still tousled from where I'd run my fingers through it.

His face relaxed when he saw I was awake. His hand went to mine and squeezed. "Lily, I'm so sorry. I didn't know you would react... like that."

I groaned from the fresh waves of pain that bolted through my body. Everything inside of me hurt like I'd broken all my bones and then put them back together again slightly different than they'd been before. "What happened?" Everything was so fuzzy. I remembered the classroom. Drinking the black vial. Then...

Dear gods.

My heart twisted when it all came flooding back and

tears sprung to my eyes. I didn't want Kaito to see me fall apart, but I couldn't help it when my face crumpled. "I'm a monster," I whispered, my words hoarse as if I'd spent hours screaming.

Kaito shushed me and immediately his lips were on mine. "You're not," he promised between kisses. "You're anything but a monster."

I suddenly became very aware that I was alone with Kaito and his hands were on me without hesitation. Perhaps it was guilt for putting me through a living nightmare, or perhaps he'd found a way for us to finally be alone without repercussion. I pulled away from him and he went to my neck, making new sensations zing through my sore body.

This must be his bedroom. Simple decorations lined the walls with more than enough books to fill a library. I felt strangely at home among the spines that piled atop one another and was the only audience to our taboo.

He was a school counselor, a teacher, and I was his monster student.

He was also my Virtue, and I was meant to be his.

That assurance made me melt into his touch and he responded to the shift in my body, forming his hands to my hips and pulling me closer to him. He ran one hand up the side of my skirt, riding the material up my thigh. He pulled away long enough to gaze at me. "Lily, let me give this to you. I can ground you. I made a mistake pushing you like that. You weren't ready to learn all of who you are, but I can help."

He was right. Every touch and kiss made me feel more myself, sane, grounded. My gaze dipped to his open shirt and I licked my lips. The sexual desire wafting off of him was intense. He wanted me more than anything right now and me looking at him made his passion even stronger. I tested the limits of our connection as I ran a finger down the center of his chest, plucking away his buttons as I went. His mouth parted.

"Lily," he breathed.

My gaze flashed up to his. "You mean Lilith," I corrected him even though the truth sent nausea through my stomach. He had to know who it was he was touching. Surely if he just realized that I was actually a demonspawn, a creature of hell and sin, then he'd save himself any further heartache. He couldn't possibly be with me if he really knew the truth, could he?

He surprised me by chuckling and my eyes went wide when his tattoo shifted colors from black to a ruby red that gleamed with magical power. "Lilith," he tested the name. His eyes started to take on that red hue as well and I watched, mesmerized. "If you're a monster, then so am I."

I didn't get a chance to ask him what he meant by that, but I didn't care when his fingers gripped possessively around my thigh and he ran one hand under my shirt, slipping under my bra and flicking a thumb over my nipple, making it harden under his touch. I gasped and he took advantage of my open mouth, thrusting his tongue over mine and sending sweet desire through my body. My succubus side couldn't feed on his lust, not with the rune on my arm, but I still drank in raw power. When I realized that it was our connection, I soaked it in greedily.

This was what it meant to be my Virtue.

It didn't weaken Kaito like I suspected a succubus feed would have. He groaned over me as if the experience heightened his pleasure.

Feeling bolder, I thrust my hand down his pants and gripped his erection, the supple skin smooth against my fingers. He bucked against my grip. "Not yet," he breathed, his husky voice puffing his hot breath against my face. He kissed my neck, then traveled with playful nips down my shirt, biting me through the fabric as he peeled it away. My bra was still an obstacle and he bit down onto it, the pressure on my nipple making me long for his tongue. "I want to show you how much this means to me," he said, his hands going to my skirt zipper at my hip. He slowly ran it down, revealing skin.

I watched him with anticipation, then nodded, giving him permission. He ran my skirt down my legs, taking my underwear with it and then his kisses were on me, making me throw my head back and his tongue thrust boldly into my folds and made pleasure explode behind my eyes. "Kaito," I breathed. I couldn't believe this was happening. With every lap of his tongue I crept closer to an edge that looked out over an abyss I'd never felt before.

I was a demonspawn who'd only known suffering and a few curious tastes of this world, but I hadn't experienced this.

I was a... virgin.

The knowledge made me blush and I wished that I wasn't. I didn't want Kaito to feel like this had to be special just because it was my first time. Would it kill his mood if he thought I was inexperienced?

When he slipped a finger inside of me, I gasped, a light tugging of pain mixing with my pleasure.

As if he recognized the distinction his gaze flashed up to mine. "Lily," he said, his lips swollen from kissing me, "is this... are you..."

A wave of heat ran over me. Before Fortune Academy, before my Virtues, I didn't know what blushing felt like. I didn't have their passion to keep me warm and I'd been nothing but a cold husk. But now with Kaito in the most compromising of positions over my sex, I flamed with heat as he asked me such a personal question. "Yes," I said, casting my gaze down, ashamed.

He lapped at me again, this time gentle as he slipped his finger out, making me squirm.

"I won't make you come for me then before I'm in you," he said, making disappointment flood through me. He grinned. "You'll be tight enough. After the pain, I will give you so much pleasure that you'll forget all about it."

He still... wanted me?

My eyes went wide as I nodded my agreement. He leaned back to peel away his shirt, then he undid his pants and his erection slipped out, making my mouth water. I wanted to taste him, but he took off his pants and then settled his hips over mine, slowly grinding his dick onto my clit. The power of that pressure made my eyes roll to the back of my head. I was so close to the cliff... if he kept doing that...

He stopped, making a sound of agonized protest escape my lips. He chuckled again. The sound settled inside of my chest and I lapped up the brush of power his pleasure gave me. "Do you want me inside of you?" he asked.

Gods, yes I did.

I gripped his hips and ground myself against him, desperate for that pressure. "Please," I said, not caring if I was begging for him now. I needed this and I'd die if he took it away from me.

He ran his dick over my slickness and slipped a fraction inside of me, making pain and pleasure spark behind my eyes. He waited for me to relax before he went just a little bit further. "Tell me if you want me to stop," he said, his breath coming in pants now. I could feel his restraint, how much he wanted to plunge into me and take me with all of the passion raging underneath the surface, but he wouldn't hurt me. He would make sure to be gentle.

I was a fucking demonspawn. I didn't do gentle.

Testing the connection within us, I found that string that connected his heart to mine and I yanked on it, hard. He gasped and his hips thrust out, pushing all of his girth inside of me. The pain hit first, but then the pleasure washed over me with such intensity that I cried out. "Don't stop!" I screamed, and he rolled his hips again, grinding blessed pressure against my clit and finally I tipped over the edge of that cliff and stars sparked behind my eyes.

I wasn't in Kaito's bedroom anymore. I was somewhere else far above the heavens, beyond hell, beyond my past, beyond anywhere Monster Academy or Fortune Academy could touch me. I clenched around his dick as he thrust deep inside of me, riding the waves of my pleasure as he fought his own release.

There would be time for more sex, I wanted him to come with me, so I stroked that connection again, making him groan as he was forced to fall over the cliff with me. Heat exploded inside of me and the sweet music of his cries joined mine.

The bond snapped firmly in place.

WE HAD sex three more times that night, each more delicious than the last. The first time was enough to solidify a Virtue bond with Kaito, but I wanted to taste everything he had to offer.

He stroked sweat-dampened hair from my face as we came down from our latest high. "The others will have felt that," he said with an amused grin.

I blinked at him. "What?"

"Your other Virtues," he clarified. "You've been establishing bonds with them already. I can sense them."

Oh. Wow.

I wasn't entirely sure who my other Virtues were, but I suspected. Logan. Hendrik. Orion. Maybe even Dante. The thought of them feeling my pleasure and a connection of a new Virtue had me blushing hot all over again.

Kaito tested his teeth against my neck as if thrilled he was the first to have me. "They'll either be coming for you hard now," he promised, "or they'll fight it. It'll be up to you what you want to do with that."

That won a grin from me. If anyone would fight a

Virtue connection it would be Hendrik and Orion, and I delighted in the idea of tormenting them.

I closed my eyes as Kaito massaged my breasts, awakening my senses for the fourth run of the night.

I'm Lily Fallen and not just a pretty face. I'm a monster in disguise and my bullies won't know what hit them.

To be continued...
Fortune Academy: Year Two

RECOMMENDED READING ORDER

All Books are Standalone Series listed by their sequential
order of events

Elemental Fae Universe Reading List

• Elemental Fae Academy: Books 1-3 (Co-Authored)

• Midnight Fae Academy (Lexi C. Foss)

• Fortune Fae Academy (J.R. Thorn)

• Fortune Fae M/M Steamy Episodes (J.R. Thorn)

• Candela (J.R. Thorn)

• Winter Fae Queen (Co-Authored)

• Hell Fae Captive (Co-Authored)

Blood Stone Series Universe Reading List

Recommended Reading Order is Below

Seven Sins

• *Book 1: Succubus Sins*

• *Book 2: Siren Sins*

• *Book 3: Vampire Sins*

The Vampire Curse: Royal Covens

• *Book 1: Her Vampire Mentors*

• *Book 2: Her Vampire Mentors*

• *Book 3: Her Vampire Mentors*

Fortune Academy (Part I)

• *Year One*

• *Year Two*

• *Year Three*

Fortune Academy Underworld (Part II)

• *Episode 1: Burn in Hell*

• *Book Four*

• *Episode 2: Burn in Rage*

• *Book Five*

• *Book Six*

• *Episode 3: Burn in Brilliance*

Fortune Academy Underworld (Part III)

• *Book Seven*

- *Book Eight*

- *Episode 4: Burn in Ruin*

- *Episode 5: Burn in Darkness*

- *Book Nine*

- *Book Ten*

Crescent Five: Rejected Wolf Shifter RH

- *Book One: Moon Guardian*

- *Book Two: Moon Cursed*

- *Book Three: Moon Queen*

Dark Arts Academy (Vella)

- *Book One (KU/Audio/Hardcover)*

- *Book Two (KU/Audio/Hardcover)*

Unicorn Shifter Academy

- *Book One*

- *Book Two*

- *Book Three*

Non-RH Books (J.R. Thorn writing as Jennifer Thorn)

Noir Reformatory Universe Reading List

Noir Reformatory: The Beginning

Noir Reformatory: First Offense

Noir Reformatory: Second Offense

Sins of the Fae King Universe Reading List

(Book 1) Captured by the Fae King

(Book 2) Betrayed by the Fae King

Learn More at www.AuthorJRThorn.com

Thank you for reading the first installment of Fortune Academy! I hope you enjoyed it and will leave a review on Amazon!

If this is the first book you've read from me, I encourage you to check out Seven Sins next. All my books are written in the same world with consecutive events and Seven Sins is where all the fun gets started. While it's not necessary to read these series in order, you'll enjoy seeing brief reappearance of characters throughout the books.

Check Out the Full Reading List at
AuthorJRThorn.com!

Read Next
Fortune Academy: Year Two

Made in the USA
Columbia, SC
12 July 2024

38349553R00145